The Age of Stupid

Folk Tales Old and New

[The folk tales are old, the telling of them is new.]

Contents

Cinderella

Prince Dave stood perhaps six feet two inches in his motorbike boots. Black leather from head to toe except for his glossy-black full-visor helmet – which had special fittings to secure his gold coronet while riding. On full-beam the motorbike headlights projected a silhouette of the Royal Standard onto the road ahead. The number plate read simply "DAVE".

Prince Dave's motorbike was blood-red and chrome – and black too, there were some magnificent matt-black bits that did some terribly clever technical motorbikey things. The wheels and tyres were so wide that the damned thing ought to have been able to stand up on its own. There was a little gadget at the front to allow the Royal Pennant to be flown, so that Dave was a royal convoy of one even when his security escort cars couldn't keep up with him, which was most of the time. The engine had cylinders all over the show, had more cubic centimetres than you could shake a small peasant at and the whole ensemble went like hot snot off a duck's back. It was a *Triumph* of engineering.

The usual reaction when Prince Dave roared past was 'Jebus H on a pogo stick, if that man wanted me to have his babies I'm about six large vodkas away from blushing and saying *I do*.'

The women of the Kingdom of Rutland were even more effusive, but with less of the babies and more of the "with a few (dozen) changes here and there (and everywhere) wouldn't he be just the perfect accessory for me in my slinky little red/black/green dress or what?" routine.

One way or another, everyone wanted to wear Dave like a hat.

Prince Dave didn't care about any of that. He just liked riding hard, up and down through the mountains, or around the lakes, or into the woods, or all three and preferably in the anonymous dead of night. When he wasn't blasting around the kingdom he liked to stop at one of the palace's lake shores and skim stones, or ride up to the top of one of the palace's rocky outcrops that had a waterfall and listen to the thunder of the cascade. Sometimes he just lay back on his bike and waited until his eyes adjusted and he could make out the Royal Milky Way in the Royal Night Sky, when all that he could hear was the tick tick tick of his bike's engine cooling down and the hooting of royal owls in the royal woods.

Dave ate bacon and bacon with fried eggs and bacon for breakfast, Marmite butties for lunch and usually an Indian take-away for dinner, and he sometimes just fell onto his bed at dawn and slept all day in his leathers. He did all of his own motorbike maintenance and he paid his own speeding fines*.

*In truth this was easier for him than for most, since Daddy's ugly mug was on all of the currency and Dave could ask the Royal Mint for samples at any time. He just rang a little bell and someone would appear with a few of stacks of tens, twenties and fifties on a silver salver.

Really, it was a lousy, rotten life being a prince in the Kingdom of Rutland, but somebody had to do it. Dave did it very well.

The King and Queen – or rather, Mum and Dad, to Prince Dave – sat on their respective thrones (they had interconnecting bathrooms) and they discussed both his future and theirs, and that of the monarchy in general.

'He's too wild' said the Queen, straining a little because of yesterday's banquet for the Dukes of Naptonshire, Trumptonshire and Midsomershire, at which some twit had served a dodgy coq au vin made with the toughest, oldest coqs and the youngest, cheapest vin. She braced herself against the gold hand-rails, and wondered, as a swift mental aside, how all of the various royal muscles knew how to work together, and in what order, inside One in the warm bluish darkness of the old alimentary royal canal.

'He's young – he's just enjoying himself' replied the King, wondering if he'd ever be able to stand up again. Where the old coq au cheap plonk had blocked and frustrated the Queen's every manoeuvre, it had accelerated *his*. He'd probably deliberately been served the unwashed arse-end of the coq in question. Bastard chef. He'd never really trusted French cooking since Waterloo. Well you couldn't, could you? If they couldn't kill you one way they'd get you by another. Murder you to death with double cream or raw langoustine or slugs-in-garlic-butter or something. In Rutland the Secret Service coveted their "double oh" rating, in France the equivalent was a Michelin Star and all that you had to do to be awarded one was to carry around "mon jamais-washed omelettes-only pan, oui?".

The Queen didn't so much reply to the King as simply continue with that age-old married couple's version of conversation; the two incidentally-interlocking but otherwise disconnected monologues.

'Well we're not getting any younger. He'll have to face up to his responsibilities soon enough' she said, dabbing at her hot forehead with a cold flannel and spraying a dense fog of extremely expensive Eau de Grimsby Fish Docks around the room. There really was nothing else with the olfactory balls to smother a feminine royal coq au vin fart. 'What would it look like if you and I were to die right now and Dave became King tomorrow?'

'It would look as though he and the chef had pulled off some murderous plot together' ventured the King, seriously worried that his arse cheeks would catch fire from whatever chemical reaction was taking place down there. 'Dear Zeus, please don't let me be the king who is remembered by history for spontaneously combusting while sitting on his private shitter.'

'What was that, dear?' asked the Queen, who was beginning to realise that she'd just have to accept feeling all day as though she'd swallowed a sack of concrete, and wait for Mother Nature to do her worst when the insane bitch was finally good and ready.

'Nothing, dear, I was just praying for the monarchy to survive this day' said the King.

'Well I am glad to hear that you're taking this seriously' said the Queen. 'We *must* take action!'

Both high-level cast-iron toilet-cisterns emptied and refilled in unison, twice. Such things happened when you'd been married for longer than most of your peasants live. The flushing had rarely been known to solve the problems that their majesties left behind during State Visits to the lavvy, but it did go some way towards preserving the patterns on the porcelain.

The Queen groped her way towards the sound of her ladies in waiting, batting the Eau de Grimsby fog aside as she went. In her worn-and-washed-to-grey-but-favourite-because-they're-most-comfortable bra, knickers, corset and bed socks, with a tab-end dangling from her bottom lip, H.M. looked like she'd staggered off the set of One Million Years B.C., Urban Geriatric Porno Redux. The tiara clinging onto her sparse pillow-hair at some brutalised angle didn't help matters, and nor did the line of stray toilet roll that trailed her every step, like some poor person's bridal veil.

In the King's Chamber a small gentleman with a large poking stick approached, nodded affably to the king and then began rolling up his sleeves, ready for battle with what he oft cheerily referred to as "His Majesty's first and most important official business of the day". The king was walking like an elderly chimpanzee wading through dense undergrowth, and if what he was wearing were once boxer shorts they were most certainly punch-drunk and ready for retirement in the old boxers' home, the one very near the crematorium.

'Christ Almighty!' said the small gentleman involuntarily, as *his* first *enemy* of *that* day hove into view. 'I'll need reinforcements Sire – send for the Army, and ask them to bring the heavy artillery and a Chaplain with battlefield experience.'

'What was that, dear?' enquired the Queen, rolling her eye (not the glass one, obviously) at her Chief Gentlewoman of the Privy Chamber and *her* poking stick. *Men* didn't half witter on sometimes.

'Nothing, my love, just the Groom of My Stool praying for an early release' replied the king.

Lady Lucinda Fotherinham-Felchingham was on the threshold between bed-chamber and the Queen's privy chamber, reaching in with the stick and waving it around, tapping as though searching for a land-mark in the fog or perhaps a guide dog in a hazmat suit. When she withdrew her hand her white cotton glove had taken on a sort of nicotine yellow hue. Collecting her nerve and holding a lace handkerchief to face she then made headway into the fog as though fencing with some unseen opponent. *Someone* had to get to the window-catches. The wallpaper was hand-printed Georgian, and the fumes had already peeled some of it off in whole sheets.

The Queen wondered if they were really such bad employers? One never knew for certain, did one?

Primped, preened, powdered, dressed and ready for *Better* Business, they then graced the Royal Dining Room with their presence, and continued to fret about Dave.

'Sometimes I wonder if he's cut out to be a king' said the Queen, poking at a devilled kidney to see if it was in any way fresh. It didn't try to crawl away, as she had hoped, but it still had a little bit of "give" and so seemed fresh *enough*.

'Well, the people already love him...' offered the King, feeding sliced white bread into the red gaping maw of the industrial toaster, watching it disappear from the human world with no promise of ever returning. How odd, he thought, that Hell Ltd should run this sort of service, toasting bread. The squealing chains and over-heated bearings sounded rather like The Damned, beginning another shift at work. The King almost forgot that his beloved, The Queen, was still talking.

'He's always running away on that motorbike of his.' The Queen cut herself a slab of scrambled plover's egg and transferred it to her plate, straining the handle of the spatula under the weight. 'Eggs a la house-brick again' she muttered to herself. Doubtless the plovers in question had been up before dawn laying the eggs, and the eggs had been going cold in the solid silver serving dish ever since. 'All that I ever seem to hear from him these days is "eat my rubber, Mummy" or "must burn dust, Your Majesty" or some such, as he accelerates across the lawn, off to fetch another ton up, or whatever the phrase is. A ton of what, exactly?'

The King couldn't argue the point, Dave was in the saddle more often than not. The King's burnt toast popped out of the machine, along with a small trident*.

*The devilish fork type, not the devilish missile type.

A scaly, clawed hand groped tentatively out of the industrial toaster, found the little trident and snatched it back inside. Then it popped out again just long enough to give the King a rather rude V-sign.

The King could have sworn that he heard echoing demonic laughter from inside the machine.

'This is no laughing matter, dear, please be serious. BALLS! Sometimes I think that he just hasn't had the balls. It's not an easy ask. He needs more balls' said the Queen rather forcefully, poking at a mushroom, uncertain whether it had escaped from a tin all by itself or whether Chef had helped.

The King assumed that odd physical expression that was half *oy vey* and half *if only you knew*. The King looked at the luxury jams on offer that morning: African Cucumber; Durian Fruit; Sweet Potato. The King looked at the luxury marmalades on offer that morning: Escargot & Garlic; Lettuce & Butternut Squash; Tripe & Stilton. He selected Marmite. 'Now I don't think we can accuse Dave of lacking in the balls department, dear. I've seen the way he rides *and* I've read the Security Service reports of his antics. Believe you me, dear, Dave's got more balls than the Coldstream Guards on "turn your head and cough" day.'

The Queen looked puzzled. 'Balls – *parties*. If we're going to tame Dave he needs a wife and to find him a wife he needs to hold his own balls. We can take a back seat, at the front of the dais on our second-best thrones, and he can invite every likely girl who thinks that she might one day be able to fill my shoes. Before you know it he won't remember what a motorbike *is* let alone that he used to love them so.' The Queen piled eight rashers of bacon (grilled until rigid and then left to go cold) onto her plate, slapped the bottom of a one-litre bottle of HP Sauce until it screamed and then began her morning nosh. 'Tell him he's old enough to hold his own balls now and that I expect him to do so at our earliest convenience.'

'Yes, dear. I'll suggest that he has a few hundred friends around for a quiet party.'

'Like hell you will' said the Queen, a stray baked bean making its way down her chin and leaving a trail of suspiciously watery, probably *non*-Heinz, tomato sauce. 'Palace would be over-run by hard-drinking rods and mockers and thumping to that *metal* music. They'd drink all of your best clarets, vomit on the carpets, and we'd be no nearer to a satisfactory secure succession solution. No,

7

we will do the invitations and *he* will find a wife from among them. How difficult can it be? We'll feel the quality, he can feel the width.'

With that the Queen slapped a kedgeree-burger between two bits of toast, grabbed her packet of twenty Silk Cut and a box of matches, and walked out through the new white-PVC patio doors into the rose garden to dead-head a few gardeners.

The King wasn't convinced, and he said so in not so many words to his kippers. 'Gentlemen' he said, 'without wishing to *harangue* you, this will end in salty tears for all concerned, you mark my words.' The kippers looked back at him like the wise old statesmen that they were, and they kept their counsel to themselves. The King ate them as he leafed through the morning tabloids.

Proclamations went out through the kingdom. "*Party party party*" they said. "*Fancy being the future Queen of Rutland?*" they continued. "*The King and Queen invite all candidates (must be biologically, politically, socially, ideologically and by popular assent female) to a BYO Big BBQ Bash at the Palace (use postcode P1 for satnav, then follow the foil-balloon trails). Next Saturday eight 'til late. Best bib and tucker. Live entertainment. No need to bring references, if we don't already know you then you're not really a serious contender, are you?*"

Perhaps two percent of the one hundred percent of the forty-eight percent of the kingdom's population who were biologically, politically, socially, ideologically and by popular assent *male* but also immune to oestrogen and curves and neoteny and females advertising their ripe status not with the bright blue and bright red bottoms of baboons, but with colourful hair instead, read the proclamations and felt their hopes dashed.

'Dash it' they said. 'Our hopes are dashed. We *had* hoped that the prince was a bona fide knob-jockey and would rule the kingdom with detached wisdom and a spot of nellie style, but no, apparently – from this information – he's just another basically decent chap being led through life by his penis's irresistible pre-programmed imperative to spray his DNA over the breeding females before any putative rivals get a chance to do so.'

Harsh, perhaps, but then their hopes *had* just been dashed, and there's nothing like a hope-dashed homosexual to put their finger on what was, you must admit, just exactly the right spot. This is why "Spot" is such a popular name for dogs.

One hundred percent of the fifty-two percent of the kingdom's population who were female, this *including* the perhaps two percent of that one hundred percent of the fifty-two percent who in reality actually worshipped at the Temple of Venus rather than the Temple of Mars, let their eyes grow wide with ambition. Queen – now there was an "up yours, Daphne", for the competition. Yes, they liked the sound of that, they *all* liked it a *lot*.

Those of the aforementioned wide-eyed group who had neither money nor position for serious palace consideration allowed their ambitions to morph into mere day-dream material, picturing themselves surrounded by their very best friends, with themselves on the throne giving everyone that look – the "How's this for ultimate status, you sad also-ran bitches?" look. Yes indeed - money and power and money and position and money and power and money and money, not forgetting power and position – and money. Oh, how their bosoms heaved still as they caught the bus to work for another day in the office, or drove the kids to school in the ageing BMW 1 Series hatchback while wearing only a pink négligée, furred-up but warm pink dressing-gown, pink slippers and tearful pink eyes.

Prince Dave and his motorbike slept apart during most of these preparations on his behalf, Dave fully-clothed as usual and face-down in his chambers, his motorbike parked in one of the many fountains in the grounds, or sometimes halfway up the front steps. Once, during a particularly dark and stormy night, he'd roared home and caught his old Nanny sleepwalking in flagrante del bent over and picking the daisies on the front lawn. Carefully nosing the motorbike's front wheel between her arse cheeks he had turned the engine off and then climbed up the ivy trellis to his room.

Prince Dave wasn't then a terribly happy prince.

He had a very bad case of must-eye seriously.

'Must I, Mum, seriously? I'm really happy just the way I am, and you and Dad are going to live for years and years yet.' [Dave had checked this with the Palace doctors.]

He was told that this wasn't the point, that the succession *had* to be secured while he could still command a high price in the wife market, while he was rich and powerful and still young enough to be behaviourally-malleable and still satisfactorily bullish in the sack. No woman wanted a husband who was rich and powerful but *old*.

Yes, all of the worldly-wise footmen in their gold livery raised a confused eyebrow at that one, but for obvious reasons none of them dare correct the Queen.

'We just want the best for you, dear. We want you to be as happy as we once were. Um – as we have sometimes been. Um - are, as happy we *are*. The King and I. One. The King and One. Happy. Now. Aren't we, Kingy dear?'

'Have you been happy, Dad?' asked Dave.

'Your mother tells me so, son, and who am I to argue? Look, it has to be done so just lie back and think of Rutland. There's really no escape. Believe me. It's The Law.'

The King and the Prince stood in the palace breakfast room for quite some time then, each separately thinking about who made such a law and why any man would bother observing it. After an hour or so of hard thinking they became aware of the sound of the Queen returning from her morning "slash and burn" constitutional in the rose garden, and they both scarpered, the King to his smoking room full of pipes and exotic tobaccos, up in the palace attic with too many stairs for Her Majesty to climb *too* often, the prince to his mews garages full of motorbikes, safely in the palace back yard among the dustbins and the servants, where Her Majesty's *social* nose would *never* allow her to explore.

Neither of them had come up with even a hint of one single real and practical reason why a man couldn't just keep on going his own way.

The day of the great ball arrived and up went the exciting PVC banners strung along the driveway and at the front of the Palace.

"This is a carbon-neutral event."

"Diversity makes for a better ball."

"Our balls are all-inclusive."

and

"To ensure *equality* all guests of honour have been selected from affirmative action all-female short-lists."

"Ladies please use the main entrance."

"Gentlemen use the tradesman's entrance (absolutely no exceptions)."

Roger, as he strung up the last of those banners, knew that this was in fact not true. He considered himself to be the eppy-tome (as he pronounced it) of a gentleman, and yet his wife had never once let him use the tradesman's entrance.

From early morning onwards aeroplanes began landing like sea-side seagulls at the Palace's private airstrip, bringing with them all manner of exotic foreign victuals (crispy aromatic koala, milk-fed mongoose, boiled eagle). Goods trains chuffed and snorted into the sidings at the Palace's private railway station, delivering hampers of food and cases of wine and – hilariously – even a small herd of live baby coypu, for the evening's stir-fry (the platters of baby-seal Wellington would have competition).

HGVs used the tradesman's entrance of course, and the palace footmen were kept on their toes, reversing refrigerated vehicles up to the flappy plastic doors of the kitchen's delivery bay where the palace kitchen maids took over with their domestic fork-lift trucks (muffled wheels) and moved the pallets to the freezers (individual pots of yummy semolina – the kind with a little sachet of sugar-free jam in every pot; tubs of fat-free Neapolitan ice cream; "no bake" cheesecake with high-fibre oatmeal-based base).

Flaming brands were being dipped and re-dipped in low-fat road tar and eco-filtered old engine oil, ready to be used to light the driveway when dusk fell that evening. The ornamental ponds and fountains were emptied, the fish tossed onto the compost heap, and the mechanisms flushed with Jeyes Fluid and then made to gush Lambrusco and Blue Nun. The ice cubes and cocktail cherries would be dumped in just before the doors opened.

Coal for the fires was delivered and pushed down the coal-chute.

Sheep and Shetland ponies and old or lame Guide Dogs and all manner of delicious dining-table mainstay were delivered and pushed down the meat-chute. Not all of them *enjoyed* the experience of landing in a heap at the bottom to await the Palace slaughterman's pleasure.

The catering butcher apologised to Chef about the order being short, but the weight, he said, had been made up with one or two ugly rescue centre donkeys who just weren't pulling in the kiddies' pocket money donations anymore.

Scullery maids with the IQ of diced tinned vegetables were made to stand with their hands in sinks of freezing water, peeling exotic fresh vegetables as they came hurtling down the palace's exotic-vegetable chute. Potatoes were skinned alive, broccoli was ripped apart and cabbage after cabbage met its end alongside hundreds of kilos of yummy turnips and tasty parsnips.

Cartridges for the evening's Lame-Duck Shoot were pushed down the Gun Room's ammunition chute.

Tame ducks, lamed especially for the evening's Lame-Duck Shoot were pushed down the Gamekeeper's *wild* game chute. Was *that* ever a mix-up! Soon sorted though, by the Gamekeeper's Assistant Assistant Assistants' Trainee Apprentices.

Oh how the staff loved their lives in the various dark cellars, preparing for huge balls!

The lawns near the palace were trimmed (by hand, with scissors) ready for games of croquet. Corridors were cleared of obstructions so that any gentlemen who (foolishly) turned up to the event would be able to play "the cricket" indoors and keep themselves out of the way of the *nice* people. Billiards tables were lowered and the pockets enlarged so that everyone (no matter how short or physically discomnobulated or how female) could go home a winner.

The great ballroom itself, where the dancing would take place, was polished from chandelier to arsehole. The floor was waxed with only the very best wax, harvested fresh and warm from the ears and the greasier parts of the orphans and urchins in the nearby workhouses; Orphawax-Urchinshine (Pat.Pending). The shine was such that you could see your own bone-structure in the reflection, like an x-ray plate. It was magical. Many an old and *overly*-inbred family's gloved extra finger or strapped-up sixth toe thought cunningly hidden would be discovered in this way that evening.

Indoor gardeners cleared a space in the arboretum where the King would later plant the special Magic Singing Ringing Snowflake Tree that would offset all of the evening's icky carbon output *and* hug a lickle baby kitten that had lost its mummy somewhere in the Amazon Rainforest. Aw – bless!

The band began to set up and rehearse and do "sound checks, yeah?" with their big bass triangles and over-amped Peruvian nose-flutes. The singer, as nervous as was to be expected and anxious to give of her best, began to gargle on the quarter hour, every quarter hour, with smoothies made from iced Domestos and loose rust flakes collected from the band's Ford Transit van's wheel arches. You can't sing dance-along feminist-folk-blues anthems without a certain amount of oesophageal scarring. Preferred pronouns me/me Yoko-Oh-No-Screechpott liked her microphones to be dripping with meaningful blood at the end of a performance (only feminist singers bleed).

The star comedian (*not* comedienne, shey/thee insisted), who had been hired to break the initial social ice, paced up and down in her *green* room (not "dressing room" since that term tended to make men – the savage bastards – think of *un*dressing and thus objectified female artists – not artistes). Shey/thee was trying desperately to memorise the new feminist-WOKE-diverse-inclusive material she'd written specially for the evening. It wasn't an easy task, due to biologically-discriminatory bastard male-pattern brain algorithms.

Ms It's Pronounced *Wul-Wah*'s work was legendary in the WOKE comedy world.

Oh how they laughed. Guffaw, guffaw, guffaw. Ms Wul-Wah virtually *lived* in a sea of jazz hands!

The only group that seemed *not* to appreciate her work was the visually-alternatively-enabled. They never applauded. Instead they just *whined* when questioned by Police that they couldn't see the sea of jazz hands and were worried that if they jazz-handed in isolation or at the wrong moment they might be thought to be being raceristish by "minstrelling". They were obviously all just humourless bastards, unappreciative of Feminist efforts on their behalf, just like everyone else (apart from Feminists).

'Cough cough' said the comedian, preparing her warm-up remark. 'Cough cough. Testing testing one two three, Mary had a little lamb, she was oppressively typecast as a shepherdess, testing testing tap tap tap whistle whine whistle is this microphone turned on? Can *everyone* hear me? Look at me – I said LOOK AT ME – alright then, I'll begin.'

'A non-binary Englishwoman of colour, an alternatively-enabled Irishwoman and a vegan-lesbian Scotswoman walked into a bar. No, but seriously – peace and love, eh? Bad-dum tish!'

'How many WOKE men does it take to change a light-bulb? No, but seriously, domestic violence *is* a gendered issue. Ba-dum tish!'

'My dog's got no nose. No, but seriously, he's got no balls, either, I had them cut off. Ha ha! Ba-dum tish!'

'Twelve nuns were enjoying the convent's communal showers after a hard day of inter-denominational, non-judgemental positive prayer when one of them dropped the soap. The Mother Superior retrieved it, rinsed it off and passed it back to her. Ba-dum tish!'

Oh god, she just *knew* that she was going to have them rolling in the aisles that night! Stardom beckoned. Even if she couldn't snag that chuffing prince she was going to get her fame and fortune.

The palace's imperfectly-formed but large army of small but perfectly-formed footmen were trying on their costumes – skinny black hot-pants, bow ties and goose-bumps. One of them suddenly snapped his fingers – the penny had dropped, landing on the other side of the coin for a change. 'I know what's going on here' he said. 'We're being objectified! Treated like nothing more than sex objects! They just want to ogle our bodies!'

The silence lasted a moment or two, and then they all went back to tying one another's bow ties, giving each other advice on how to avoid leaving chest hairs in the soup, and the correct etiquette to follow if it was the Queen who had her hands down your pants towards the end of the night.

Throughout the kingdom scraggy old munters were getting their daughters ready to attend the event of the century, hoping beyond hope that at least *they* would do better than some fat, lazy, insufficiently-wealthy minor earl or petty baron. Feminist Godmothers went into over-drive and the better sorts of houses were awash with unicorn-fart sprinkles and with pixie-dust. Daughters were almost suffocating under the weight of attention.

'Darling, I don't care if you can't breathe. Breathing isn't the point. You can breathe once *you're* queen and when *I* can have your father executed and I can move out of this grotty little manor house and into a fully-serviced apartment in the palace.'

'Yes, mummy.'

Next household...

'Alright dear, give me your best smile... oh for crying out loud! Alright, don't smile, not ever – you look like a spaniel with freckles and trapped wind. Hide behind your fan and try to emphasise your child-bearing hips. He's not going to be marrying you for your smile, dearest, that much is evident. Put some *thrust* into that pelvis – you have to convince his mother, the Queen, that you can produce male heirs like some human Gatling gun.'

'Yes, mummy.'

Next household...

'Belinda you *can't* wear that backless dress, there isn't an ounce of fat on you, you look like a xylophone made from ribs and covered over with skin from a plucked chicken. No there's no time now to begin eating anything, you ought to have thought of this years ago before you went onto the Atkins. You'll fall into the orchestra pit and someone will begin playing tunes on you and before you know it you'll be married to a penniless musician. No, we will go, no arguments, with the all-over tiger costume. Just don't trip over the tail and, when you growl try to make it a "come to bed, my Prince" growl – not as though you're a stray cat begging for a saucer of milk.'

'I suppose so, mummy. Grr? GrrrRRR?'

'No dear! Like a tiger! Like a tiger!'

'Yes mummy. Ger-owl! Ger-owl!'

'No! No! Grile! Grile! You must be a *Home Counties* tiger, not some feline slut purring on an outhouse wall in the provinces! One must *grile*. Grile! Grile!'

'Yes mummy. Grr-grr. Grr.'

'GRILE! GRILE!'

'Grr? Grr?'

'I despair of you, Belinda, I really do. So much at stake and the best that you can come up with is to sound like a mildly annoyed hedgehog.'

'Sorry, mummy.'

Next household...

'Mummy? The riding outfit or the fancy-dress dominatrix?' 'Is there really any difference, dear, apart from the size of the whip? Whichever is fine, dear, men can't resist a woman who smells of either horses or leather and you always smell of both so you're quids in. Your father and I just wish we understood – it's not as though we *have* any horses.'

Next household...

'Daddy, does my bum look big in this dress?' 'Ask your mother, dear – she has my opinion.'

'Mummy, does my bum look big in this dress?' 'Bloody enormous dear, and you'd need solid steel knickers to smooth out that cellulite, but you will insist on eating. Still, men do like something to get hold of, all is not yet lost. Christ, I just hope that the elastic holds when you curtsy. I have this terrible picture in my mind of you bobbing back up and leaving those vast canvas knickers of yours around your ankles. You'll *have* to wear a pair of Daddy's trouser-braces under everything, otherwise I'll be hospitalised with stress before the night's out.'

Next household...

'Lucinda, darling, you look *perfect*! What man can resist skin-tight nylon leggings, a low-cut slightly-dubiously stained baggy top from a charity shop rack and comfortable hiking boots? On a substantial woman, I mean.'

'Yeah, what*ever*, mummy.'

Next household...

'Hyacinth, we've just got to emphasise all of your good points while disguising the flaws. We'd better start with the disguising first, just in case we run out of time. Do you still have that floppy wide-brimmed hat with the very, very heavy veil, the one you wore to your grandmother's funeral? The one that made you look like some sort of beekeeper-in-mourning in a silent closed order of very shy nuns who worship god by keeping out of the sun?'

'Yes, mummy.'

Next household...

'Muffin, dearest, Daddy and I don't care if you're a – what did you call it? A *lesbian*. This is the chance of a lifetime and if Prince Dave wants to screw your brains out on the dance floor or even in the trifle bowl you will, and I repeat *will*, thank him and fake an orgasm. Then you'll tell him that you're pregnant. It's the way I caught your father and if it's good enough for me then it's certainly good enough for you. Now, elegant white satin with the Velcro-release knickers, or the full fairy princess rags with crotchless tights and ballet-shoes?'

'Sniffle.'

'*Do* stop crying, dear – once you've married him and got the title you won't ever need to sleep with him again. It's just a *pretend* marriage, dear, and you can go back to doing whatever it is that you do with – what's her name – with that nice Miss Bulldyke Todger-Dodger. Is she one of the Sussex Todger-Dodgers, dear? Anyway, just go through the motions darling, snag the prince and it will all be over soon and you can get me that knighthood for your father that he's somehow never quite managed to get for himself.'

'Oaf uck, mummy. I suppose so. Ce sera sera.'

'Sarah-Sarah? But everyone always calls her Bulldyke. Sarah-Sarah Todger-Dodger. No, I don't think she's one of the Sussex branch. Your grandmother would have told me if she were, she knows all about absolutely *everyone* worth knowing. Anyway, darling – these crotchless panties – tell me that you *have* done a little bit of work in the garden recently, haven't you? It runs in the family dear, and whenever I'm lax about using the shears your father always complains that I look as though I'm being attacked by a short-legged nocturnal omnivore of the Mustelid family. Won't come near nor by, says it would make him feel as though he were the badger-buggering Bishop of Bath.'

...and on and on around the county, the county set were girdling the fruit of their loins, so to speak.

The fashion "industry" certainly pushed the envelope that night. In fact it licked the envelope, put a stamp on it and sent it off to La-La Land. Some of what would be seen in Rutland that evening would stamp itself indelibly on the observers, never able to be unseen.

Came the hour came the King and Queen to the impressive front steps of the castle to meet and greet (and to assess and to admit or to deny) their guests. The arrangements were not too formal, just the usual three miles of red carpet from the inner Palace gates, H.M. K and H.M. Q on the top steps on informal thrones with a sea of hand-made Indian rugs around them and a crescent of armed flunkies behind.

Eight until late, the invitations had said. At half-past eight their majesty's were becoming a little bit worried. Had they advertised the correct date? Had the roads leading to the palace been closed by the local council for pot-hole repairs or something? Had the guards at the Outer Outer

Outer Gatehouse forgotten to take the chain off the gate? Had the event clashed with the high-drama climactic final episode of a televisual "soap" opera set in some ever-cheery, crime-free square of London? Had the event accidentally coincided with an exhibition match of the ever-popular international women's football; a floodlit, packed-stadium evening of tears, tantrums and mixed emotions?

A senior flunky checked on each count. 'No, your majesties, it's probably just everyone trying to be fashionably late. Take a chill pill and don't be such a pair of precious panic-pansies.'

H.M.K. and H.M.Q. took the flunky's pithy advice. The Q assumed that any flunky *that* rude *must* be one of the K's favourites, and the K assumed that the Queen was just testing him, and refused to be drawn into whatever game it was that she was playing.

'Who - or ought that to be whom? Who-whom is One expecting to come, dear?' enquired the King, not really giving a shit but knowing that life would be both easier and quieter if he feigned interest – and that he might as well kick off events, thus getting himself to the final whistle sooner than just sitting around and waiting for the argument to begin.

'Oh, the usual crowd. I do hope that they've made an effort this time thought. I've had Dave fed on nothing but oysters, bufo toads and horny goat weed for the past week, so he ought to be gagging for a shag' replied the Queen, painfully aware that the King wasn't a social creature and was wearing his striped flannelette pyjamas under his dress uniform, the quicker to get to bed – alone - once his evening of torture was over.

Dave was far from gagging for a shag.

Dave was just gagging.

Dave was, in point of fact, in his chambers and hugging the Great White Telephone, wondering when he'd eaten all of these Brillo Pads and diced carrots and whether they'd ever stop coming back up. There wasn't a power on the planet that might induce him to let go of the cool, cool toilet to go downstairs and dance the night away with a load of *prospects* chosen by his mother. 'Hugh-eeeeee! Raaaaalph!' he cried, and the soon-to-be-promoted flunky who was holding Dave's chest hair out of the way and making sure that his coronet didn't fall into the toilet pulled the gold chain to flush, again. Two gallons of House Rosé swirled around and then disappeared around the u-bend. Dave's gratitude knew no bounds, the man was a life-saver. How fantastic the splashes from the toilet flush felt on his face!

Isn't it just amazing how something that is more ordinarily regarded as dirty and horrid can become such a huggable thing of comfort when your body is hell-bent on launching the contents of your alimentary canal into space?

Someone knocked gently on the bathroom door and indicated that H.M.K. and H.M.Q. had enquired after Dave and wondered when within the next thirty seconds or so or *else* that he would be joining them on the receiving line of the ball.

Dave slipped his wireless portable telephone from his back pocket, took a "selfie" with the toilet and the mysterious carrots and the less-than-mysterious Chinese-supplied oysters and then tossed the phone to the King's man. 'My reply' said Dave, turning then once more to peer down the u-bend for signs of his immediate future.

The King showed the photograph to the Queen. 'Food poisoning?' he suggested.

'Social bulimia' replied the Queen. 'He's just being dramatic. Your mother was just the same. He gets it from *your* side of the family.'

The King was puzzled but said nothing. Like all royals they were so in-bred that there *were* no distinct "sides" to the family. 'Mi grandmother es su grandmother – and grandfather *lived* on a bicycle' thought the King, although bright enough not to actually vocalise the point in present company.

The Queen addressed a senior flunky. 'Assign someone to vomit on Prince Dave's behalf. Have his little royal highness washed, tushypegs brushed, mouth rinsed, dressed and here in five minutes. Use some of the old cattle-prods from the Royal Nursery if needs be. He always did respond well to those.'

The first guest, Lady Harper Bassington-Bassington, arrived in an *electric* Austin Princess (which was towing a trailer housing the diesel-generator plant that powered it once it had exhausted its three-mile battery range). A discreet little chrome badge on the bonnet pointed out that the car was an ideal first limousine and was quite suitable for teenagers of all shapes, sizes and IQs.

Harper found herself in immediate difficulties, attempting to remember how to open a car door for herself. This was because the palace flunkies all took their cue from the King and Queen, who had used their Magic Marker pens to write "Hybrid is so last year, dear" on large cards and were holding them up. Harper, it appeared, had blown it before her new shoes had even touched the red carpet. Climbing out of the window of the Austin she ran – in tears – up the also-rans' side-steps, to one side of the main entrance.

Lady Annabelle Foxhunt-Killiekillie, whose Daddy owned television, delivered herself via a very large LED screen, a Skype link and a specially-launched satellite dedicated solely to ensuring that Annabelle's image arrived safely at the ball with absolutely *no* carbon footprint from any icky travelling at all on her part. Unfortunately, a love-rival whispered anonymously in *everyone's* ear in re the carbon footprint of the *satellite, and* Annabelle's father had sold advertisement time on Annabelle's channel, so sometimes Annabelle was in (a corner of) the ballroom, sometimes it was Pedigree Chum's New Chunky Chipmunk Chunks or some Gillette #metoo lecture for men on how men really ought to be better women. As ball arrivals went it was a case of "nice try, somebody please hit the mute button and pop an antimacassar over the screen in case the budgie lands there and takes a shite".

Annabelle – in floods of tears – ran then up the staircase in mummy and daddy's place, which was even *further* away from the palace's main entrance than the official also-rans' side-steps.

It wasn't long before Television-Annabelle was hijacked and hooked up with some of Prince Dave's (bored) best mates, one of these best mates being something called "a games console" by Daktari Ltd of The New Japanese Empire. Annabelle's eyes crossed as she watched – with not some little virginal horror - the approach of the HDMI cable.

The official scoring for her arrival was "Aw – bless! Norfolk'n'chance. Thanks awfully for the spare television though. Tootle-pip."

The later guests seemed to do better in their eco-feminist-SJW-snowflake-minnelliumnal virtue signalling modes of arrival.

Lady Oriana Bagsamoolah-Butnosense had put her heart and soul into her mode of arrival, as per the instructions on the reverse of the printed invitations sent out by email. Oriana arrived in a bio-degradable pumpkin-shaped cardboard coach pulled by six examples of the near-extinct species "Giant Panda" – all of them female, of course; no self-respecting Feminist would be pulled along by *male* pandas!

The pandas were a bit seriously scarce to be honest, so one or two of them had to be persuaded to "self-identify" in order to make the power-plant all-female. It's amazing what a panda will do if you just shove a bit of bamboo up its nose.

Oriana was buzzed out of the receiving line for "unmitigated cultural appropriation" (the pandas being Chinese and Lady Oriana only being Anglo-Celtic-Norman-Saxon-Viking-German-Roman herself, and none of this counting one iota in the more-ethnicityerishnous than you stakes). There then ensued an unfortunate skirmish between the dray animals and the footmen, one of whom was eaten during the fracas, even though he looked nothing like bamboo and had very little up his nose.

'Oh fracas!' Lady Oriana was heard to say, not bearing to look at the King and Queen who were shaking their heads (heads still attached at the neck, unlike that of one of their footmen).

Remember, children; pandas are wild animals and are dangerous, so never never never leave a valuable footman within reach.

Lady Oriana, also in full floods of salty tears, ran up the side-steps and into the ballroom and dived straight into the punch bowl where she stayed until she'd drunk it dry and would then have wrestled everyone, had she been able to get up the slope out of the bowl. Wham bamboo thank you ma'am. Hic. Gemmyacoffee, black.

Lady Delphine-Yah Countreh-Countreh, a comely girl of generous proportions and with few psychoses worth mentioning (now that she'd lost her gun licence), saw the problem with the coach-and-pandas but judged it too late to withdraw, she being next in the arrivals on the palace driveway's now blood-red carpet.

Poor (stinking rich, atcherly) Lady Delphine was in a *bamboo* litter being carried by two very hefty and also endangered Mountain Gorillas (again, female, of course). In truth it was difficult to decide what it was that was endangering the gorillas most – the destruction of their mountain habitat in whatever foreign piss-hole of a country it was that they were native to, or Delphine's material pact with Mr Gravity. It must be noted that it *is* unusual to see female Mountain Gorillas wearing professional weight-lifting belts and sweating like pigs.

The Queen sighed and looked to the King. Was there to be no end to this cultural appropriation? How might One express a blown raspberry and hoots of derision on an arrivals score card?

'Nerrrrr-errrrrrr.' H.M.Q. went so far as to mime pulling a lavatory chain.

The pandas, being down-wind of the bamboo litter, caught thus the wind of a feast, and an almighty brawl ensued in which Lady Delphine prevailed but after which several more endangered animals had bitten *the big one*. It was an entrance, certainly, but a highly risky one.

Upon seeing the fight that Delphine put up – albeit a fight motivated on her part by the simple impulse to retain her limbs and to continue living – the Queen revised her score and allowed Lady Delphine to enter the ballroom via the front door, with a smile (and with a First Aider).

Leaning in confidentially to the King, H.M.Q whispered 'Now *she's* a possibility. Did you see the way she punched that gorilla? I'd like to see what *she* could do with a coconut.'

The King had no doubt that Lady Delphine was proficient in several methods of cracking coconuts bare-handed, bare-kneed and probably also using just her eyebrows. 'Her forehead, dear – a little Cro-Magnon, do you think?' he replied, diplomatically.

'Well if it's the *Buckinghamshire* Cro-Magnons she's not a *first* cousin, so everything ought to be fine, really. If she wins tonight then we'll have her checked before we breed from her. If the DNA's too close a match we'll breed Dave from one of the gorillas instead.'

The Cinderella household had pushed out all of the stops with their marriage applications. Um – I mean *with their arrivals* at the palace for the Big Ball. They were *so* green that it hurt your eyeballs to watch. It didn't get more eco-aware or right-on-yah than they. You couldn't have made a bigger or greener splash if you were an intact bull-elephant and you'd dipped your bollocks over-enthusiastically into a vat of Forest-Mint matt green emulsion at the Dulux factory shop-floor Christmas party.

Lady Nasturtium Cinderella and Lady Gorgonzola Cinderella (their mother had suffered dreadfully from nutritional urges before she finally dropped the twins in the dining room at The Dorchester) arrived to much applause. Lady Nastie, as she was known among her staff, arrived on a skateboard propelled by outboard-swan farts. Lady Gorgon, as she was known among *her* staff, eventually, very eventually, rolled up by means of an exhausted Loggerhead turtle strapped to each foot.

'Oh how lovely!' cried the Queen. '...and you've brought roast and a soup too!'

'Such *practical* girls!' the Queen confided to the King in a whisper, via his (purely political) ear-trumpet.

'Yes, indeed' replied the King, thinking that the taller one, perhaps, with handlebars glued to her head and a saddle strapped to her back might resemble a primitive sort of motorbike and have at least an *outside* chance of attracting Prince Dave. The shorter one might, just might, he supposed, appeal as something to lean a motorbike up against should the stand ever fail.

As they curtsied the King leaned forward to them. 'Can you make noises like a double over-head cam variable-valve-timing in-line triple being revved in a confined and echoing space, such as a royal bedroom?' he asked.

Thus it was that Lady Nasturtium and Lady Gorgonzola entered the by-then crowded ballroom with puzzled expressions, and making "putt putt PUTT" and "brrm brrm BRRRMMM" noises, but not really understanding why.

The other guests, thinking this to be a quite splendid thing to do, all joined in.

One or two of the old colonel types (Dame Colonel Hilda Schootefirst-Grenadelater D.S.O., and Dame Colonel Evadne Nighs-Gnockers O.R.E.) made startlingly accurate "burble burble" noises, and some of the younger debs, not knowing what a motorbike was, just blew continuous raspberries.

The palace staff had quite a bit of damp then to wipe off the walls and windows; the upper-crust lips of the gentry aren't always the best-controlled of human appendages, especially when wobbling in the lower frequencies.

Prince Dave, reasonably certain that he'd ejected all of his oysters, chose that moment to appear on the ballroom steps. *Very* Busby-Berkeley, but then you've either got it or you haven't. Dave both had it *and* had had it. It was bad enough his parents inviting all of these hypergamy-harpies to the house for him to choose from, but to get them to sound like eager little mopeds ripe for the riding too... My god, there was one who actually *might* pass for a smaller Triumph – if someone glued handlebars to her head and strapped a saddle to her back! Prince Dave couldn't though, for the life of him, understand why she might have had a Loggerhead turtle strapped to each, already more than ample foot. Presumably this was the latest fashion in feminine footwear.

A helping hand from behind pushed him down the stairs, and he arrived at floor level more in the manner of Des O'Connor at The Palladium than of Barry Sheen stepping forward to accept a Lifetime Achievement Award.

The Conductor did his best to help, but half of the orchestra gave a resounding "ta-daaaa and For He's A Jolly Good Fellow" while the other half, thoroughly confused and woefully under-paid at the best of times, played the first few bars of Happy Birthday To You. A certain melodious ...awkwardness... ensued wherein the conductor picked up his spare baton and tried to conduct using both of his hands simultaneously for different tunes. After eventually stabbing himself in both ears he tapped in stereo on his music stand for bloody silence.

Some wag in the gathering of the dance floor took the opportunity of the moment's quiet to make a very passable "screeching of tyres followed by a crashing into trees" noise.

Another imitated an ambulance siren attending.

No-one felt Dave's pain. In a room jam-packed to the ceiling with the one half of the species that supposedly held a monopoly on preternatural empathy, compassion, and the milk of human kindness, Dave was utterly on his own with his feelings. The black-uniformed, peaked-cap, jackboot-wearing, monocle-squinting members of the Patriarchy Oversight Committee who were in one corner watching over proceedings, looking for any – *any* – signs of Patriarchal Society breaking down, nodded sagely and made satisfactory notes on their clipboards.

Finally recovering themselves the assembled *debs* curtsied as one. There rather suddenly wasn't a length of knicker-elastic in the whole room that wasn't sore tested. Prince Dave took the opportunity of the lowered heads to turn to try to run back up the stairs, but was foiled again – curses! – by the sound of the door to the private suites being locked. The orchestra, feeling a touch of the axe about the back of their necks, sashayed then into the Rutland National Anthem (Pulp version).

Cinders Cinderella, having sneaked out and followed her big sisters to the ball, lurking in the shadows and keeping her smelly, rag-a-muffin distance, took this as her cue. She had arrived at the palace during Dave's embarrassment, and she had arrived in the green greeny greenest possible manner; on foot and wearing leaded-glass thigh-boots made from recycled windows salvaged (nicked) from medieval churches while they were being demolished to make way for ticky-tacky housing developments. What better way to preserve a little bit of history?

It should be noted that Cinders was wearing other items of clothing too, not just the glass thigh-boots. Her sartorial ensemble had also been "salvaged"; Cinders had spent almost an hour hand-sewing together some old tea-towels and a pair of asbestos oven-mitts into a sort of too-short toga dress with a floor-cloth & mop motif.

The ballroom, as one, un-curtsied and backed away, clearing a path between Cinders "The Kitchen Scrubber" Cinderella and her feller. This wasn't out of respect for either the prince or for Cinders (certainly not for Cinders), but because with every step that she took the assembled party-goers could hear glass splintering, and they were afraid of flying shards. Nobody wanted to die of up-cycled medieval glass stiletto-heel to the forehead or a leaded peep-toe bow through the throat.

Cinders advanced, step by crunchy step. Agony was no longer just a distant aunt writing problem page columns for wimmin's magazines.

The band continued with the pulp version of the Rutland National Anthem.

Cinders didn't want to live like common people. She had no intention of ever again doing whatever it was that common people did – although there *was* a touch of the Greek about her upper lip, and she certainly had a thirst (although not, in her case, for knowledge).

An experienced mobile flunky served her an octuple rum & generic sugar-free cola in a pint glass with a handle, no ice, no umbrella.

In her heart of hearts Cinders knew that she'd won. Won won won. Forget your Surrey Cro-Magnons, forget your farting swans and your bio-degradable cardboard coaches pulled by unicorns or terrapins or whatever it was. Cinders stood just so, one hand on hip, her pint in the other, and she pouted while the band segued into some ancient 78rpm era classic track about Those Boots not being Made for Walking.

'...but that's just what they're going to do' thought Cinders.

Just as she opened her mouth to sing at him Prince Dave ran.

He ran like the wind.

He ran faster than the wind.

He ran as though the Devil herself was chasing him which, when you think about it, she was.

Dave ran right around the palace to the stable block, leapt onto a motorbike, *any* motorbike, and roared off into the distance. Burble burble burble said one or two of the Absinthe-sipping, lorgnette-unfolding old dames, as they watched him roar back around the palace and past the ballroom windows into the evening. Those who could still get their arms above their shoulders made the respectful sign of the Ape-Hanger Handlebars and gave a few twists of the Holy Throttle.

Cinders felt as though her hops and dreams had been shattered. Her *hopes*, too.

Flunkies under orders from H.M.Q. gave chase, armoured cars were commanded to charge hither and thither, footmen followed him in motor-bike & sidecar combinations and it was hopeless – for Dave. Even the mountain gorillas and the pandas joined in the hunt. He found himself cornered, trapped against the wide barbed-wire fence at the front of the palace's private gardens, the sovereign state of State Marriage on one side and the Republic of Freedom and the snow-topped mountains on the other. Short of options, Prince Dave roared his motorbike back and forth a few times, checking out the lie of the land, and then he gave it the beans and very nearly, quite absolutely almost, made the leap over the fence.

He lay helpless while the uniformed forces approached, and indicated his surrender as best he could.

It took a while for the Palace Firemen to cut Prince Dave and his motorbike out of the tangled barbed-wire and anti-tank arrangements.

His great escape, his last and admittedly ill-advised attempt to go his own way, was over.

Henceforth, whenever there was mention of palace balls, someone would bring up the subject of The Great Escape, and everyone would watch the DVD again whether it was Christmas Day or not.

Prince Dave was taken by private ambulance to the local R.H.S. Accident & Emergency Unit, and there he lay, beaten and vulnerable, on a trolley in an ill-lit corridor, waiting for an over-worked locum to be sober enough to see him. Like all such patients, Prince Dave counted the holes in the polystyrene ceiling tiles.

One, two, three... eight hundred and twenty-two... nineteen-thousand and fifty-six...

Note to H.M. Mummy and H.M. Daddy; please *significantly* increase the funding for the Rutland Health Service, and put pictures on the ceiling in all of the corridors and treatment cubicles.

Just when Dave had classified and catalogued the holes in the ceiling tiles as well as counting them all someone in hospital greens and a three-day beard hove up and giggled at whatever it was that was written on Prince Dave's patient record clip-board. Then she kicked his trolley down the corridor, through the swing doors and into a curtained cubicle. Dave's time had come. The green plastic curtains hid well the pus squirted from previous patients, but the blood gushes had all dried to a sort of icky-brown colour. Dave was put in mind of the shower curtain in a B&B he'd once stayed at in Cleethorpes.

Once they'd cut his leathers off, his beloved leathers, the nurses dabbed his wounds with something that stung like hell. It was nothing to do with being anti-septic, the yellow solution was nothing of the sort, it just stung like hell, and was fun to use on male patients. The nurses all placed bets on how stoically he would take the pain. Then, when he finally looked as though he'd been making mad, passionate love to a box of razor blades *and* had splotchy jaundice, and was thus fit to see a doctor, the nurses drew back the curtains around his cubicle. Some of the crusty bits fell off (the curtains, not off Dave).

Quite unexpectedly, angels sprinkled the moment with fairy-dust, and a unicorn galloped through the room (with a cork on its horn, of course – health and safety needs must when the Devil rides out). Somewhere in another cubicle nearby a "last stages" consumptive tuned in a small transistor radio to a station that played romantic cinematic orchestral music (Der Ring des Nibelungen played on the saxophone, mouth-organ and bongos).

There, in the very next cubicle to Dave's, on the very next shit-stained rusty trolley, under the leaky hiss of the very next piped-oxygen wall-socket, lay Cinders.

A fluorescent lighting tube lost its grip on the ceiling at one end, dangled by the wire and threw a quite magical localised glow onto her positively elfin face.

Both of her feet were raised in slings, and they had been bandaged until they were the size and shape of footballs that had been bandaged with too much bandage. Here and there the bandages leaked not some little blood, and the left one was beginning to show streaks of pus. Cinderella tried to lever herself up on her pillows, and she smiled a weak, what-a-brave-soldier-we-are smile.

'What? What happened to you?' asked the Prince, in the vice-like grip of emotional messages from his head, emotional messages from his heart and, most importantly of all and being impossible to ignore, emotional messages from his cock.

"The poor unfortunate wee thing – a *lady* in distress" said his head.

"I must save her at all costs from the possibly entirely unintentionally less-than top-notch ministrations of the cash-strapped and over-burdened R.H.S. – save save save" said his heart.

"Woof woof woof" and "awoogah awoogah awoogah" and "twice missionary and once doggy-fashion just for starters" said his cock.

Prince Dave silenced his head and his heart, and listened intently for Cinderella's reply.

'What happened? Oh – my glass boots. I may have won the carbon-neutral arrival contest, but I also learnt that a girl ought never to stamp her foot petulantly when she's worked so hard on her entrance and yet her prince storms off on a motorbike into the night. Left foot cut to ribbons. It's like raw tripe and red onions in a cheesecloth sausage-skin down there.'

'But – but you've got *both* feet bandaged...' said Prince Dave, drowning in wave upon wave of his portion of human dimorphism instilled and buried deep under the blazing sun of pre-history and evolution. Sympathy sympathy sympathy, save save save, protect protect protect, shag shag shag came the instinctual cave-man waves, with frothy, foamy white horses at their rolling tops.

Dave's Reason & Reality Gland, quickly putting such of its affairs as it could still reach in order, muttered something about "told you we ought to have taken the homo option", and then it died for ever. Mourning would last a lifetime, but it wouldn't begin for weeks yet, maybe even a month or two, and it would only peak after the split with the palace and then the inevitable messy divorce.

'*Both* of your poor ickle-bickle footsy-wootsies...' said Dave's mouth, reading from its new script, composed entirely of sound-bites from Hallmark Cards for Toddlers.

'Oh, yes. I broke the other one getting into the boots in the first place. It's not easy getting into glass boots, especially leaded medieval glass high-heeled thigh-boots.

The fracture was complicated and they tell me that something smelly called "gangrene" has set in. I don't think that you men realise how much we girls must suffer for fashion, you know, just because we know that you like us to look our best for you.'

Cinderella gave a little wince of pain and repeated her best weak smile, allowing her saline drip tube to drop provocatively into plain view.

Dave's Reason & Reality Gland came back from the dead, briefly, just to mutter about how "naked and carrying beer would have done as far as your average heterosexual bloke was concerned, and all of this bollocks about gangrene and saline drips was just gratuitous over-kill".

Prince Dave, as helpless as a new-born baby that lay in the ruins of its favourite motor-cycle leathers after trying to crash through a barbed-wire and anti-tank fence, felt that he was trying to contain some nuclear explosion in his guts.

The unstoppable mix of emotion and instinct and unreason and lust and training and social expectation (and a last rumble from the bad oysters) grew and grew and grew until Dave could contain it no more. The whole process of changing from fully-independent adult man to enslaved fool took about two seconds.

Prince Dave swore – out loud – that he would love her until the end of time.

'Cinders, I swear that I will luvvy-wuvvy-wuvvy vu until da end of time, yeah?' said Dave's mouth entirely without reference to or approval from what little remained of his conscious brain.

So, yes, Prince Dave is now waiting impatiently for...
THE END (of time).
Cue the music.

Pinocchio

Pinocchio was a broken man. No, I mean literally broken; his cell-mate had snapped him in half and was using one of Pinocchio's legs to make matchsticks and the other for a wood-carving of the Virgin Mary for the prison chapel. Pinocchio was miserable. He lay on his bunk – well, the top half of him, anyway – and ran his tin mug up and down the bars. Life is shit and then some bastard snaps you over his knee and takes a pen-knife to you. There had been some mutterings about "and a fruit bowl out of your head, later" too.

We get ahead of ourselves though. Much had happened to Pinocchio in the one month, two weeks, three days and four hours since the five minutes of his marriage ceremony, and little of it had been recounted (or ruled as admissible) in the six minutes of his murder trial.

It all began not so very long ago in a country not so very far away. The country was called Gynocentria, and it was sort of southern European Mediterranean *"continental"* in its national outlook. The summers were hot with cooler moonlit nights, and the winters were perfect for uphill skiing to gentrified shepherd-huts with roaring log-effect fires and steaming outdoor Jacuzzis. The people of Gynocentria were a very, very passionate and demonstrative people. At the very least provocation the mothers wept, the fathers cried, and the children flicked chins and bit knuckles and ran numbers and drugs and weapons for the Gynocentrian equivalent of the old Italian Mafia.

The Muffia as it was known, ruled supreme. The Godmother had only to kiss a chap on both cheeks (face-cheeks, usually) and he was toast. The Godmother, in certain lighting conditions (these being daylight, moonlight, candle-light, electric light, the cold light of dawn, police camera flash-light, and The Light of Creation), looked very much like Marlene Brando, and she spoke – when she spoke – with a certain accent and a measured cadence. Occasionally she coughed wads of cotton-wool from her cheeks and when welcoming supplicants into her presence she often made hand gestures with more gravitas than those of the Pope gesticulating to the crowds from a Vatican balcony.

Gynocentria was a wonderful country. It had a fine and crinkly coastline with sandy beaches and an azure-blue sea, it had vineyards where grapes sunbathed nude and drank nectar from the soil, and it had beautiful mountains where lonely goat-herds often hitched up their lanolin-stained smocks and interfered with their flocks at night. There *were* big cities of course, even one with a traffic-light controlled road junction, but most of the Gynocentrians lived in picturesque little towns with big and ornate fountains, and with vast, ancient churches and houses that had been passed down through generation upon generation (of solicitor and estate agent and mortgage-broker).

Family was very important in Gynocentria. There were two kinds of family. The first, although it was of secondary importance, was your typically extensive collection of mothers and fathers and brothers and sisters and aunts and uncles and cousins and grandmothers and grandfathers and great-aunt-sister-cousin-uncle-mothers and the great-great-aunt-sister-cousin-mother-aunts. The second family, much more important than the first, was the Muffia. In Gynocentria, if you hadn't kissed the Godmother's ring you were nobody.

Mouthwash was a very important part of the Gynocentrian economy. It was produced in red wine and in white wine flavours.

Pinocchio had only the very basic, "starter package" first-family – just an old wood-carver, called Mr Old Woodcarver. Woodcarver was a very popular surname in Gynocentria, and Old was as much an honorific as it was a boy's first name. Not many men lived to be old in Gynocentria, there were too many shoot-outs with the Polizia, and too many honour-killings carried out by the Muffia. If someone's elbow spilled your morning espresso or afternoon cappuccino then you were honour-bound to either pay to have them whacked, or to whack them yourselves. If a chap was under eighteen then it was fine if his mother did the whacking for him. Mothers take their laundry seriously in Gynocentria, and coffee doesn't half leave a stain on wide-collared open-necked shirts and beige Crimplene slacks.

You can't sprawl effectively on a classic Vespa scooter with coffee stains all over your ensemble.

Bloodstains though weren't a problem, but were in fact a badge of honour (but only if human blood – sheep's blood didn't count).

Pinocchio didn't imagine for one second that he would be able to get married and build a *proper* family for himself. Pinocchio thought that he was betrothed in perpetuity to his right hand, a tin of Ronseal Hardwood Garden Furniture Oil, and a copy of Wood-Turner's Pictorial Monthly. He watched other little boys grow up and get married and have twelve children and six stomach ulcers and a suicide involving an un-registered WWII hand-gun and a knackered old Fiat parked in some lonely disused marble quarry, and he was sad. Would his day ever come? Would *he* ever come if the Old Woodcarver kept getting to the copy of Wood-Turner's Pictorial first and tearing out the pages showing well-carved naked piano legs or pairs of voluptuously rounded finials side by side?

So it was that one day after rather enthusiastically watching their amply-proportioned next-door neighbour, Signora Bucatini coi Funghi, bending over in her garden to pull the weeds, Pinocchio wiped his hands on an old rag dipped in turpentine (nothing else got the Ronseal off), and he went outdoors to sit in the shade by the old town fountain and to be sad and lonely and post-mono-coital.

The kindly old town Priest, Father Fettuccine Alfredo, noticed Pinocchio sitting there, looking so sad and lonely, and he went over to try to comfort him, as priests often do.

'Pinocchio, Pinocchio, are you not worried about damp rot, you stupid little fool, sitting so close to the town fountain?'

Pinocchio looked up, and there were splashes from the fountain in the corners of his eyes. 'No, Father, I have been pressure-treated with a good-quality preservative, and I ...I oil myself regularly.'

'Why so sad then, my little fencepost?'

'Father – I am scared that I will die a virgin, like some sad old town priest.' Pinocchio tugged absent-mindedly at a splinter in the heavily-scarred palm of his right hand.

Father Fettuccine Alfredo puzzled for a moment over who Pinocchio could be referring to, but then he remembered that as a priest *he* was supposed to be the one with the factory plastic wrappings still on his genitals. It really was amazing how extraordinarily insensitive people could be when talking to priests. Christ, the faithful could *really* hurt sometimes.

'There's nothing to worry about, my son, and no rush at all. It will happen when it happens. God is good. How old are you? Seventeen? Eighteen?'

Pinocchio looked up at the priest. 'I'm one hundred and thirty-seven this year.'

'Merde!' said the priest, not wanting to sully his own language and knowing that the French wouldn't mind. 'You have left it all a bit late. Are you... I mean... does everything still work, down there?'

Pinocchio stuck his legs out and waggled his feet. 'Oh yes, Father, I have double-pinned joints and there's very little rust on my hinges.'

'No, no, my son – I mean, could you keep a woman happy?' asked the priest.

'Give her everything she asks for, you mean?' replied Pinocchio.

'*Something* like that, my son, yes. Well, for example, how would you support a woman?'

Pinocchio thought for a moment. 'I'd get one with legs of her own, then she could support herself' he said. 'I like legs. I use up a lot of Ronseal oil thinking about legs on ladies.'

The priest wasn't unaware of the female leg himself, and he thought that the answer, although not quite what he had been looking for, had a certain merit.

'And, of course, in terms of personal fiscal structural integrity, I shall inherit Old Woodcarver's business one day. One day soon. He has... inoperable woodworm.'

The priest thought for a moment and then the divine light of inspiration lit his face. He looked like a tortoise coming out of hibernation and finding that its neighbourhood had been overgrown with several varieties of tortoise-favoured lettuce. He put his hands together and offered silent thanks for the inspiration to the patently non-virginal Virgin-Mary-in-the-Sky.

'Gina! Let me introduce you to Gina.' Father Fettuccine grabbed Pinocchio by the *left* hand and dragged him across the piazza to the pavement café, where Gina was trying to drum up some trade. She was leaning against a lamppost with one knee up, and there was a very well-established spider's web between her thigh and her calf. The spider living there considered himself lucky to be largely sheltered from the rain and to be so very rarely disturbed. Gina had been trying to drum up trade since the day that the Fiat Topolino had given way to the Fiat 500. In truth, business hadn't been great for Gina since the rectal prolapse in the late nineteen-fifties.

'Gina – this is Pinocchio. You and he are to be married. Pinocchio – meet Gina. Gina Lobbabrickia.'

Gina struggled a little, detached herself from the lamppost (those well-established spider's webs can be tough, very tough – almost like steel cable), smoothed down her very wrinkly skin-tight dress and looked Pinocchio up and down. Taking a cigar from her – well, nobody knew where, she just produced things like cigars from secret places about her body – she struck a match behind Pinocchio's ear, and blew a smoke-ring at him. Pinocchio's head was about level with Gina Lobbabrickia's unfeasibly wide hips.

'I don't know' she drawled, in a voice that would have graced a growling bear. 'He's a bit small... what is he? A clothes peg?'

The priest pointed out that Pinocchio was made of rare teak and mahogany and had ivory teeth – a full set (a novelty to Gina in her line of work) - and that he was due to inherit a thriving business and a substantial freehold property any day now.

'Who am I to resist the direct orders of the Holy Absolute Patriarchy?' responded Gina, warming to Pinocchio. She bent down (at about ninety degrees), showing Pinocchio a cleavage that looked like an assemblage that ought, by rights, to be under the back ends of a couple of neglected milk-cows conversing, and she kissed him on the top of his head.

Pinocchio giggled and came in his pants.

Who would have thought it? What were the odds? The very first woman who hadn't fended him off with a broom-handle and threatened to get her brothers to attack him with lighter fuel, tinder and two bits of flint, and she was the love of his life!

The spider, being wise to such matters, hopped down from Gina's hot stock-in-trade to the hot pavement and crawled back up the relatively cool lamppost, considering the web-foundation possibilities of the broken bulb fitting at the top. It would be as well to rebuild somewhere high up, out of the way – the Gynocentrians were an effusive and effulgent nationality, there was bound to be some sort of outbreak of emotion over this betrothal. Streets were often cleaned during outbreaks of emotion.

Father Fettuccine Alfredo, overcome with the need to express his emotions effusively and effulgently, leapt onto the parapet of the fountain and began to sing about how love was a many-splendored thing. Once the priest had finished and received his applause, young Focaccia al Rosmarino, who sported a quiff, had a toothy grin and wore drainpipe trousers, took up his guitar and sashayed through a few classic and well-known Cliff Richard sing-along numbers from the nineteen-sixties. He began with *I'm leaning on a lamppost* and then, when he'd got the assembled population of the town warmed through, led them into *Grandad's Flannelette Nightshirt*, *Our Fanny's Gone All Yankee* and *With My Little Ukelele in my Hand*. Everyone danced and was happy, and Gina took a quick inventory of the Old Woodcarver's business and property, and read his medical records to confirm inoperability.

The wedding took place the following Saturday. Everyone agreed that Gina looked absolutely ravished, although Pinocchio seemed to be in some sort of pain (the smoke-trail fly-over by the National Air Force hadn't been cheap). In lieu of a father figure, one of Gina's best and most faithful regular customers took her up the aisle, and not for the first time if you'll pardon the expression.

Something in blackest black widow's weeds sat at the back of the church, knitting handcuffs from barbed wire – this was Gina's mother. Most people mistook her for a dusty shadow in the corner until she slipped the collection plate into her bag. She spat at Pinocchio's feet as he took his new bride out into the rather unforgiving light of day. Gina's mother didn't have a name; she was too old and crabby for a name, and too small, having shrunk over her years to be only just tall enough to hit a man where it really hurts. One glance at Gina's mother told you that she'd had more violently-squashed testicles on her forehead than she'd had hot goat-lasagne. As a Short Bruiser for the Muffia a dented forehead was as much a part of the job as was psittacosis to a budgie-smuggler's apprentice.

Pinocchio's bright orange Piaggio three-wheeler vanette looked magnificent, all decked out in white ribbons and straining under the weight of confetti and rice. In Gynocentria it was the custom to not throw rice loose, but to leave it in the hundredweight sack as an offering to the couple for when times became hard. Pinocchio lifted his new bride into the cab, and politely closed the door of the cargo box when her mother had stepped inside. Oh, how happy they would be!

Pinocchio was shocked upon discovering how many things he had to do while the three of them were on honeymoon. He had to visit his solicitor to make out a new will and last testament. He had to visit his bank to put Gina and her mother onto his personal and business bank accounts, and get the bank to issue each of them a new cheque book and debit card. He had to call in at the Insurance Agents, and take out a policy on his own life for one million Gynocentrian guineas. Gina's mother said that it was The Law. There was shopping to do and new furniture to buy and, because (according to Gina) the hotel was full and only had separate rooms for them all, he had to cry himself to sleep, too.

Pinocchio and his new bride never did get a chance to play *How's Your Father* even once during their honeymoon – Pinocchio just couldn't bring himself to give her more than a peck on the cheek because there was always some pile of discarded black clothing in the room that looked as though it might be Gina's mother, staring disapprovingly. It always in fact *was* always Gina's mother, staring disapprovingly. Every corner of every room in every building in Gynocentria was haunted by a tiny, black-clad Gynocentrian mother or grandmother or great-grandmother or great-great-grandmother. This too was The Law, and wooden stools were provided for them to sit upon.

Perhaps, Pinocchio thought to himself, things would be easier when they got home. He could install a child gate at the bottom of the stairs or something and at least keep the mother-in-law out of their bedroom.

Gina wouldn't go home. Gina didn't want to live over the shop. Gina wanted that nice big house on the mountain top. Gina announced that she and her mother would stay in the hotel, thank you, while Pinocchio went back to town and arranged it.

Pinocchio went to see the mortgage broker who operated on the same street as the solicitor, bank, and insurance agent that he'd had to visit earlier in their honeymoon. The APR appeared to match Pinocchio's telephone number, but he consoled himself that at least once they moved in to the mountain-top house then Gina would probably let him do sex on her.

He bought the house. They moved in. A man from the removals company carried Gina's mother indoors, and set her down in a wall niche in the hallway, having mistaken her for some sort of example of South American tribal whole-body shrinking, or some such horror. He screamed and ran away when Gina's mother said '*Grazie*' and lit up a cheroot.

Pinocchio was overjoyed to see the arrival with the rest of their furniture of a vast new King-sized bed complete with memory-foam mattress, four-poster canopy and electro-vibrate tilt and swivel controls. 'Oh what sweet, sweet memories they would give that mattress!' he thought.

Pinocchio was less than overjoyed to see his own little old single bed with broken springs being installed in a small room at the back of the house near the kitchens. Gina explained that it wasn't for long, darling, just until he got over this snoring thing of his. Rested women were so much more likely to produce babies and Gina did so very much need to rest after that lovely but exhausting honeymoon.

The only glimmer of hope on the immediate horizon was that Pinocchio later saw Gina putting an adjustable spanner neatly back into its appointed place in his tool box, and washing oil and grease off her hands. How could he possibly complain if he had a *practical* wife? Practical wives were *such* a *rare* blessing! In time they would probably be able to enjoy doing household repairs together, and perhaps some elementary plumbing.

Gina kissed Pinocchio on the head. She seemed to be fond of his head. In reality it was just too hard on her back to bend down further to kiss anything else. She was contemplating attaching some sort of swivelling handle to his ears, and maybe a hook in his back to hang him up with out of the way. 'It's too chaotic for me to cook, darling – pop down to the Pizzeria and get us something delicious for dinner. Oh – and mother likes anchovies on hers.'

'Kinky!' thought Pinocchio, as he got into his three-wheeled Piaggio van, pulled the starter cord and clattered out through the gates in a thick fog of tired two-stroke smoke.

Pinocchio felt that he had little to complain about.

He had a beautiful wife – a *practical* wife, a fantastic job in a business that he would own soon enough and a house on the top of the mountain! What more could a man want, aside, perhaps, from getting to do big sex? He determined to enjoy the drive up and down the mountain, relishing the hairpin bends and the echoing tunnels. Pinocchio wore his shades, and he sang "Questi giorni quando viene il bel sole..." to himself and life, all things considered, felt good – even in the road tunnels where he had to swerve around several inconsiderately-parked bulldozers and a couple of shiny jet-black Muffia Fiat Dino Coupés.

Pinocchio made a mental note to adjust the brakes next time he serviced the Piaggio, they were a little on the spongy side. He was so busy though commuting up and down the mountain and putting in long "catch-up" hours at work that he completely forgot about it until the following weekend.

That Friday evening, after he'd laboured the Piaggio up the precipitously steep inclines in first gear and at seven thousand rpm, he found Gina in the garden, using her mother as a marker-peg while she staked out a large and complicated shape on the grass. If Pinocchio had been bright enough to see the arrangement from space, as could the crew of the International Space Station, he would have recognised instantly the slightly impractical outline of a vast unicorn being ridden Ben Hur style by a much larger than life outline of Gina's mother.

'Poochy woochyski' she greeted him in a faux-Russian accent. 'I've been thinking about how to protect your investment in our house – a swimming pool! I've made the arrangements, you just need to take care of the nasty money.'

As Pinocchio got himself horizontal on the driveway – to adjust the Piaggio's brakes – the number plate reminded him of the APR that he'd already agreed to with the mortgage. The brake cables seemed to have stretched a little. It was probably just the heavy use they got each day as he screamed down the mountain to work.

Pinocchio had a sleepless night, worrying about finances, but he hadn't the heart to say anything – yet – because Gina got up early specially to make him coffee and breakfast before he went to work. As he entered the kitchen she was just putting away the spanner and about to wash her oily hands. Perhaps she'd been adjusting the percolator?

Pinocchio might as well have ridden a bicycle down the mountain to the shop, he had to pump the brake pedal continuously to drag the speed of the Piaggio down ready for each hairpin bend. He was more worried about the money for the pool though than about the brakes, those just needed adjusting again to take into account the stretch that he obviously hadn't accounted for when last he adjusted the brake cables for stretch. That would have been the previous evening.

All week Pinocchio sailed down the mountain on a wing and a prayer, and then slogged back up, hoping that the little engine wouldn't die and leave him rolling backwards or something. That next Friday evening when he coughed and spluttered into the driveway there was a sleek, vast and, frankly, incredibly gorgeous-looking new Fiat 130 Coupé in the driveway. Pinocchio whistled and stroked it. It was baby-blue and it shone like a jewel.

Gina opened the front door of the house to greet him.

'Gina – who are our guests? It's not the Muffia is it? The Godmother?' Pinocchio couldn't remember if they had any decent-vintage mouthwash in the house.

'Guests, Pino, my darling? Oh – the car! No, no – I was worried about being here all through the long days while you're away on business in the family car. If anything happened to Mama we would be trapped. I knew you wouldn't mind. It's only a Fiat, and I just got a two-door because we don't need the expense of four doors, not until the babies come. The dealer was ever so sweet about everything, and you just have to go in next week and sign a few papers.'

Only a two-door Fiat, thought Pinocchio to himself. Just about the flashiest, most expensive Fiat in history, the Fiat with the Pinninfarina style and the luxury – and the price-tag – although sadly not the performance - to rival any Maserati or Lamborghini. Sign a few papers, she said, just to sign a few papers? What? A contract with The Devil?

The sale deeds for a kidney? There wasn't enough money in Pinocchio's little wallet to fill the Fiat's windscreen-washer bottle with water.

As Pinocchio drove down the mountain to put some extra hours in at the wood carver's shop he found himself having to use the Piaggio's handbrake before each corner. That stretch in those brake-cables was getting worse, he'd have to service the whole thing soon. Why, he wondered, did Gina always seem to have a ruddy spanner in her hands and oil on her fingers? In the three weeks that they'd been married he hadn't found any evidence of her changing a tap washer or adjusting a door-hinge. Maybe she'd been tinkering with the washing machine? That would be the explanation, the spanner would have been to adjust something on the washing machine. Something oily and covered in road-dirt, on the washing machine. She really was the best wife a small and naive wooden puppet could hope for!

That next Friday evening when he slogged back up to the hill, exhausted from putting in twenty-hour days in the workshop and four hours sleep over his lathe (which was usually still turning), Pinocchio was surprised to find a man in the house. A very well-built, tanned, toothy and overly-groomed man, walking out of their en-suite bathroom and wearing only a very small towel, a towel that looked about as secure as a politician's promise.

Gina explained that since Pinocchio had been preferring to spend most of his hours at work rather than at home with her, she had noticed that he'd not had time to maintain the pool and garden as well as they ought to be, so she'd hired a combined gardener-pool-boy. Rather than pay for him to travel up and down the mountain each day it was much more economical for him to live on the premises, no? Was she not being both practical *and* economically-minded?

The combined gardener-pool-boy's towel dropped as he walked away along the upstairs landing, showing two tanned arse-cheeks as rock solid as cannon balls.

Pinocchio wasn't happy, and he made the mistake of saying so.

It took Pinocchio quite a while to sweep up the shattered remains of the dinner service, and he had to take time out of his work to bandage his head and tend to the other cuts and bruises. Gina's mother watched him, sitting on a stool in the corner like some black-shrouded gargoyle. When he'd finished cleaning up the debris she spat on the floor at his feet, slipped off her stool and went through to her granny-annex, slamming the door as best a three-foot-tall wraith could slam anything using just pure contempt and hatred.

Gina was ignoring Pinocchio, and spent most of the rest of the weekend out by the pool, laughing and horsing around with the pool-boy. Boy! He was twenty-five if he was a day (age, IQ, *and* shoe size). On Sunday evening Pinocchio saw the overly well-combined pool-boy returning an adjustable spanner to Pinocchio's prized tool-box, and while Pinocchio was pleased that he had obviously been doing something practical, he asked him not to borrow his tools without asking first. The pool-boy wiped the grease from his hands on a rag, walked past the lawnmower and dived into the pool to do some lengths. Tanned, muscled, graceful, young bastard! Young, hung and full of come

-to-bed eyes whenever Gina was around.

Gina glared at Pinocchio from an upstairs window, and then turned her gaze to supervising the pool-boy, to make sure that he was doing his lengths in a properly workmanlike manner.

On Monday, just before the hour before dawn, when Pinocchio headed down the mountain to put in all the hours that he could at the workshop, he found himself having to open the door of his Piaggio three-wheeler and poke a foot out to use as a brake. Even the handbrake cable was saggy – all of this mountain driving was *really* not doing the brakes any good. By the time he got to the bottom of the valley he'd had to throw the contents of his tea-flask over his foot because it was smouldering. That was one of the disadvantages of being made of wood; marital friction was your enemy.

It wasn't a good week for Pinocchio. Business was booming – because he spent most of his days and nights working at it – but he just couldn't keep up with the bills. They'd only owned it a fortnight and already he'd missed six payments on the Fiat – Muffia Finance Ltd sent him a horse's head. Not the horse, just the head. It had been on the workshop doorstep when he got to work. The town's tailor was pressing for a bill for something itemised as "tailored speedos", apparently the latest thing in gardener's uniforms. There had been a note from the bank manager telling Pinocchio that he was sad to see him go, but his savings account had been emptied and closed and he was welcome back any time he had some money, p.s., you have seven days in which to clear the overdraft on your joint current account, after which the matter will be placed in the hands of large men in dark suits and who wear black sunglasses even in winter.

That next Friday, as Pinocchio was labouring up the mountain in his Piaggio three-wheeler, he had to take drastic action to avoid the Fiat 130 Coupé which was speeding down the mountain, driven by a large man in a dark suit and wearing black sunglasses even though it was winter. To stop himself rolling back down the mountain while the Fiat passed, the progressive tactics of pumping the pedal, using the handbrake and poking a foot out of the door onto the ground having progressively failed, Pinocchio threw out a small anchor and chain. Financial and work pressures or no, he really *had* to get under the

Piaggio and sort out those brakes a.s.a.p. or, preferably, a.s.a.p.o.e.s. - even sooner.

When Pinocchio pulled, eventually, into the driveway there was another man in a dark suit also wearing black sunglasses, and he was driving a JCB, filling in the unicorn-shaped swimming pool with earth and rocks. The digger arm of the JCB was emblazoned with 'Pool Repossessions' in big letters, and in smaller letters 'Seizing luxury from bankrupt losers since 1837'.

Gina was at the front door, her mother lurking to one side. Pinocchio had no idea why but he formed the impression that Gina's mother, black-clad from three-foot-high head to toe, was packing heat and was just itching to use it.

As he got out of his little vehicle, Gina threw a brick at him (having already decided to return to using her maiden name; Lobbabrickia).

Pinocchio, having cleverly caught the brick on his forehead, popped it under one wheel of the Piaggio to stop it rolling away.

'You BASTARD!' shouted Gina, lovingly. Behind her, "Cassy" as he was known to his mates (short for Casanova), the pool boy then with no pool to look after, was stacking their luggage. He appeared to have dressed himself in one of Pinocchio's smart business-meeting suits. Having made a neat pile of things he popped Gina's mother on top, just to make sure that they didn't forget her. 'Everything's gone – the pool, my car... and even your little bank account is BROKEN!' screamed Gina, also lovingly.

Gina wept into her divorce lawyer's arms, and a crude dot-matrix printer chundered somewhere dark and a narrow till-roll receipt for "billable hours and services" extended out of the lawyer's arse: Item 272a, Client Hug, 300 Gynocentrian Guineas. The lawyer looked as though he might soon need to change the roll of paper for a fresh one.

'Where the ruddy hell did *he* come from?' thought Pinocchio. Perhaps he was inflatable, like a lifebelt, or perhaps Gina had rubbed her mother and made a wish?

Gina's mother, atop the luggage, chin-flicked Pinocchio and spat at his feet again. Cassy put her into the passenger seat of the Piaggio, loaded the luggage, the lawyer and the lover (himself) into the rear and closed the van's door.

Gina swept past Pinocchio, with just time and sense to say 'I'm selling the house now that it's full of bad memories. You can keep the mortgage. Mother and Cassy and my lawyer and I are going to a hotel while you think things over and move out.'

With that she leapt into the driving seat, pulled the starting cord like a pro and was revving the little beast out through the ironwork gates. The wheel-spin sent the welcome-brick flying back to hit Pinocchio on the head for a second time, reminding him of something.

Skull fracture? Yes, but that wasn't it.

Concussion? Yes, but that wasn't it.

Profuse bleeding? Yes, but that wasn't it.

Suddenly he remembered.

He ran forward.

'Gina! The brakes! The brakes aren't too good – watch the brakes! I think that the cables have been stretching!'

Gina, her little black widow's weeds-clad mother, her luggage, her lover and her lawyer made it around the first hairpin bend of the descent. On two wheels, but they made it. The look on Gina's face was something between that of the Mona Lisa and Munch's The Scream – she'd *remembered* too. She waved the adjustable spanner out of the window in her oily hand, but nobody understood, it was too late for anyone to re-tighten the retaining bolts that tensioned the cables, and the brakes were no longer interested in working. Damn those patriarchal, misogynistic spanners, just damn them all to Hell!

The drop from the second hairpin bend was a clear three-hundred vertical metres. Pinocchio calculated something like seven point six eight seconds to impact. Something black fluttered away as the car sailed out over the drop, either a large crow or small widow taking slow wing. A portent, possibly. Two hundred and seventy-six point zero five kilometres an hour; a personal best by the Piaggio although, to be fair, all previous attempts at "maximum velocity" *had* been made on the level. The Piaggio Owners' Club, Speed Records Division, was unlikely to ratify the feat – which only goes to show that when *women* achieve something amazing the world just isn't interested. Had a *man* been at the wheel he would have had a laurel-wreath around his neck before he hit the ground.

Pinocchio was still standing between the ironwork gates of Gina's lovely mountain-top house with repossessed swimming pool and no car in the garage when the Polizia arrived some three hours later. The Polizia all drove Alfa-Romeo Giulia patrol cars, and so had been forced to push them most of the way up the mountain.

Gina had almost survived the fall, dying only when Casanova had landed on her – the briefest but far and away the best love-making of their affair. Young chaps are easy on the eye but they are so *gauche*, aren't they? Gina's mother was never found, and being so old and frail, it was assumed that she had broken up in the turbulent air of the fall into pieces too small to find. The divorce lawyer walked away without a scratch of course, landing on his feet with his briefcase in hand, and it was he who had walked into town to fetch the Polizia.

Lawyers don't like walking. His bill, already stupendous, became STUPENDOUS. The figures were so long that he had to change the little dot-matrix printer to print them lengthways on the till-roll, since they would no longer fit across it.

The Piaggio hadn't fared well in the crash. It took simply *ages* to collect the pieces and to assemble the brakes, the stretched brake cables and Pinocchio's spanner into the evidence the Judge wanted and had been looking for.

That Pinocchio hadn't even taken out an insurance policy on Gina, while she had insured *him* for a million, spoke volumes to the court about how much she loved *him* and how little he must have really loved *her*.

Evidence was heard, not because it was admissible but because gossip was always interesting, of Pinocchio's financial troubles, how Gina's little baby-blue Fiat 130 Coupé had been repossessed, how the swimming pool had been filled in, how far behind Pinocchio was on the mortgage payments and about just how many hours and days he chose to spend at work rather than with Gina and her lovely mother. He wasn't paying his bills, so what had he been doing with their money? Another woman, perhaps several?

'Bastardo!' said the Judge. 'The evidence before this court is incontrovertible, there's no need for the jury to retire. I must throw the book at you: clearly controlling and coercive behaviour; constant domestic abuse and mental violence and, finally, murder – multiple murder most foul.'

The lawyer coughed, significantly.

'Oh yes' the Judge added to his summation 'and you tried to murder a lawyer, too – an unspeakable act in Italy. I mean in Gynocentria, an unspeakable act in Gynocentria. Unforgiveable, absolutely unforgiveable.'

The jury of strange little creatures, all short and dressed in black widow's weeds, clicked their knitting needles and nodded.

'DEATH! DEATH MOST HORRID! STRIP HIM NAKED AND THROW HIM TO THE WOMEN OF THE TOWN!' pronounced the Judge, banging his gavel until splinters flew.

A Court Official whispered in the Judge's ear.

'LIFE IMPRISONMENT!' spat the judge, correcting himself on a minor point of the sentencing guidelines. 'SEND HIM TO GAOL FOR ALL ETERNITY!'

And so it was that Pinocchio, *still* a virgin, found himself locked in a cell with Gus (short for "Gustavo di Amoré con Massivo-Loveprod"), and with Gus's whittling knife.

Lying on his bunk (already sans his legs, one of which was then in a niche in the prison chapel, carved into a statue of the weeping Virgin Mary), Pinocchio was dismayed to see Gus taking delivery of a paper bag of oranges, lemons, limes, pomegranates and coconuts from the Red Cross Parcels Office. Gus had hinted that he wanted Pinocchio's head for a fruit-bowl, and his need would be all the more pressing after this delivery. Indeed, rolling over, Pinocchio found Gus already contemplating his cranial proportions (with a tape measure, a set of callipers and his thumbs held at arm's length).

'Head for a fruit-bowl?' said Pinocchio, wiser then, and resigned to his fate, again.

'Fancy one, with a lid.' confirmed Gus. 'Going to carve naked women all around the outside. Big-breasted women. Women with breasts. Big-breasted women with big breasts. Just like-a-mama used-a have.'

'Lovely. Torso?' enquired Pinocchio, anxious that nothing be wasted, wood of his quality being rare and expensive.

'Place mats and drinks coasters; an order for the Prison Governor' replied Gus. 'Place mats and coaster decorated with women. Big-breasted women with big breasts.'

Pinocchio nodded, but then remembered what it was that had got him where he then was (in a pile of trouble), and the only part of him not yet allocated to some work of art or domestic utility. 'Penis?'

Gus smiled, and his gold tooth caught the sunlight filtering in through the grimy, wired-glass window. 'Yes I think so, one last time, while there's still enough of you left' said Gus, neatly folding his arrow-patterned trousers over the edge of his bunk, sending his tighty-whities and hernia support to land around his ankles, and reaching for the big squirty-squirty jar of chilli-infused linseed oil.

'Oh – you meant *your* penis. Ah - toothpick', said Gus, reaching out with his big, hairy hands.

The moral of the story, children?

Well boys, that would be that the cock that was already in the cell when they pushed you in and locked the door is not the one that got you into all of this trouble.

Girls – it's not for a male author to say, but if pressed I would intimate that if you are going to stretch a chap's brake cables a little each time he annoys you (by merely existing), then do remember to take a taxi when you, your luggage, your mother, your lover and your lawyer flounce out towards town to begin divorce proceedings.

Rapunzel

Rutland's really big Big Rutland Forest is lush and green and packed full of magnificent tall oaks. The forest is a million million million dozen square big miles of woody paradise. It is also packed full of magnificent, tall, wandering, woody lumberjacks.

Well, there's *one* such, anyway, and his name is Dave.

Wild wolves and bellicose bears had been re-introduced - to the landscape, not to one another – and they roamed free and hunted at other's expense, but that didn't worry Dave. Last time that a bear had tried to eat Dave he'd dodged, sparred with it playfully, punched its lights out and left it in a compromising (and vulnerable) position draped over a tree-stump with a small bunch of wild flowers poking out from whence no bunch of wild flowers ought to poke. Wild wolves, not being so green as they were cabbage-looking, soon learned to recognise the commands 'sit' and 'fetch' and 'roll over' and 'play dead'.

Dave's surname was Tallyho-Chocksaway, but there weren't many people about in the Rutland Forest to use it, and those that there were about generally just blushed and found themselves lost for words when he passed by, his huge axe slung casually over his sage-green English tweed gilet covered shoulder.

Dave walked up hill and down dale in the woods all day long most days and sometimes far into the night, selecting and chopping down trees as he went, and dragging them back to his wood-yard. Dave was built like a brick shit-house.

One day Dave was exploring an especially distant, little-visited corner of the forest, looking for an especially old and gnarled oak that he could fell and make into a new table especially for his mother's dining room in her granny-annex attached to his several up, several down, now with outside spiral staircase tower home. 'Especially' was

Dave's use-it-more word-of-the-day from his Correspondence Course. He was already sick of it, and he had secretly read ahead to tomorrow's word.

Anyway, he had just leapt ten feet across a pellucidly clear and sparkling stream when he stopped, and he put his head on one side in the manner of a dog listening to a metropolitan millennial snowflake parroting on about climate change, multiculturalism, diversity and the price of skinny soy-coconut lattés in imperially-minded coffee-shop chains. Dave could hear screeches and wailing – pellucidly some animal was in pain! Either that, or Rutland's first (and hopefully last) "Bjork feat. Ono" concert was underway. No, quite pellucidly it *had* to be an animal being torn apart!

Dave thundered into action, shinning up a tree and carefully determining in which direction the animal lay, rather than just running off through the bracken, clueless, like some impulsive "social sciences" loon. Dave knew his onions alright. In fact, he was on very familiar terms with all kinds of allioideae. Allioideae had been Dave's favourite subject in his allotment gardening correspondence course of the previous year.

The wailing was awful, the animal sounding as though more in some dreadful psychological distress than in physical pain. Perhaps Bambi had been orphaned again – it happens sometimes, you know. Father Nature has a cruel, cruel job to do and we're really quite lucky that he has the balls to do it.

The sound came from a large glade in a small valley wherein a large tower stood. Dave hopped from branch to branch as he descended from his vantage point, landing with a controlled thud that made earthworms for miles around close their eyes and reach for the Aspirin. He set off at a healthy joggy-sprint. It had been some years since Dave had been awarded a *Distinction* in his Jogging &

Running correspondence course, but one never forgets, does one?

The tower was quite without steps, the only openings being triple-glazed, UV-resistant white PVC multi-fold full-width doors on each side right at the top, giving access to a veranda that ran all around the tower and then twice back the other way just for good measure. Dave tut-tutted at the shortcomings of the architectural design. It was all frippery and little substance. Granted, the stone-work itself was decent, but who in their right mind would put a poorly-supported and *flat* roof on a tall building in a temperate zone island climate subject to the whims and caprices of both a major oceanic current *and* a wildly-fluctuating jet-stream?

'I say – may I offer any assistance?' bellowed Dave up towards the balcony and the open windows.

The wailing ceased, but nothing much else happened for so long that Dave, having shifted from one foot to the other and then found a rock to sit upon while he waited, decided that there was no-one home. Rapunzel, upon hearing the mellow baritone of Dave's voice bellowing from bellow, had rushed to her bathroom mirror to check her hair and make-up, and to re-arrange her ample bosom in what was really a terribly revealing but still vaguely medieval-style dress. Having waited for a visit from someone such as Dave for years and years and years she finished off with some eye-shiny Shiny-Eye eye shine drops, a spray of Eau de Unicorn Fart into the air and which she then walked through, and a clean pair of knickers. By the time she got to the balcony and looked down Dave was on the edge of the glade, about to disappear back into the forest.

What an annoying man, Rapunzel thought, to call unannounced and to then not wait for her.

'Woo-oo! Cooey!' offered Rapunzel delicately, waving her handkerchief and fluttering her eyelash extensions. 'Woo-oo! Hee-elp! Hee-elp!' she cried and then swooned, throwing herself over a sun-lounger that she had placed there for just such a purpose, each and every day all through most of what had been her high-value dating years.

Dave paused, turned and took a few steps back to the tower. There was no-one in sight of course, but he *had* heard a voice, possibly one being imitated by an Australian parrot-in-distress – woocooeywoohoo heelp heelp.

Dave whistled, as one might whistle to amuse an Australian parrot, and then tried a wider conversational gambit suitable for psittacoidea, cacatuoidea, and strigopoidea. 'Who's a pretty boy then? Pieces of eight, pieces of eight. Peter Piper picked a peck of pickled peppers. Sally sells seashells by the seashore. The shells Sally sells are surely from the sea.'

Rapunzel, developing a kink in her lower spine, came to realise that "swooned behind a balustrade on a balcony fifty feet above her long-awaited but conversationally-challenged rescuer" did rather put her out of his obvious line of sight, and it made communication a little more difficult than it already seemed it might prove to be. Damn her lack of spatial awareness, just damn it to discriminatory patriarchal STEM hell! She levered herself up off the sun lounger, straightened her clothing, dabbed at her hair and checked again that her bosom was firm and plump and on the verge of falling out of her dress.

'Oh bugger!' she said, as she leaned over the balcony. Damn geometry and damn perspective and all of those other Patriarchal tricks! From this far above the ground she couldn't tell whether her rescuer was tall or not. He looked *sort of* handsome from this distance, but for all that Rapunzel knew he might be built like a chimpanzee recovering from childhood rickets.

'Are you in trouble?' shouted Dave, through cupped hands.

Rapunzel was instantly incensed. Her blood boiled, her piss fizzed, and, were it not for the fact that her boiler hadn't been stoked in years, steam might have whistled out of each ear.

'BASTARD! YOU MEN ARE ALL THE SAME! I HAPPEN TO BE A VIRGIN, THANK YOU VERY MUCH' replied Rapunzel, naturally taking the worst possible view of things. '*NICE* GIRLS LIKE ME *DON'T* GET INTO THAT SORT OF TROUBLE, YOU FILTHY-MINDED BEAST!'

Honestly, a girl carries just a few extra pounds and men feel authorised to ask if you're pregnant!

'No, no – I just meant that I am sure that you *are* a virgin, and *is there something that I can help you with*?' ventured Dave, wondering what he'd got himself into and why he was bothering when there were trees to be felled and lumber to be stacked and a new table made for his old mother to sit at while she ate her twice-daily dish of old-person's cold cabbage compote with prunes.

More innuendo! Rapunzel fumed and plotted revenge. Why do men only ever think of one thing where women are concerned? Here she was in need of a simple, romantic, fairy-tale rescue from pampered, care-free and secure life in a high tower and all *he* could think about was helping to get her *into* "that sort" of trouble! Rapunzel was quiet, trying to decide whether it might be worth it.

Dave waited a few seconds and then said 'Oh, alright then. No worries, sorry to have disturbed you, I'll be going now. Work to get done, that sort of thing.'

'COME BACK!' screamed Rapunzel. 'COME BACK! OH PLEASE DO COME BACK!' Aware that she'd almost blown it before whatever it was had really begun, Rapunzel turned on the waterworks, releasing floods of salty-magic tears that no man in the whole wide universe could possibly resist. The Rule Book said that there was *nothing* more attractive than a woman in tears.

Dave wandered back to the point at which it was least uncomfortable to turn his head upwards and converse.

'Jebus H Christ – you look like a panda bear after a punch up the schnoz!' his mouth-gland said, before his manners-gland could stifle it.

Rapunzel stopped crying and then dithered in that state where either her head might explode with fury or she might begin crying for real. She couldn't decide which would be best for her.

'Sorry! So sorry! That was rude of me. It's just that your mascara appears to not be waterproof. Here, use my nice clean, freshly laundered, starched white cotton only-for-show handkerchief to wipe up those tears.'

Dave considered the trajectory, the height of the balcony and the slight cross-wind in the glade, selected a suitable stone, tied his handkerchief around it and lobbed it up.

Instead of catching it like any bloke would have done Rapunzel simply went cross-eyed as the well-intentioned missile approached her and she indeed took it smack in the schnoz.

She hit the sun-lounger again, more genuinely involuntarily than with planning aforethought this time. Rapunzel's brain struggled with formulating instructions on how to uncross such brutally-crossed eyes. Were it not for her ears pulling for all they were worth, one on each eye, she might have spent her life then looking at either side of the bridge of her (battered) nose.

'Oh for cryin' out loud' said Dave, under his breath. 'Are you alright? Did you catch it?' he shouted.

Rapunzel leaned out over the balcony, a little trickle of bleedy-weedy edging out of one nostril.

'Near enuth, yeth, thank you, I'th fine. Tho kind of thuu to athk.'

Dave was a pragmatist at heart, and keen to help where he could even if it was just to help someone understand some little detail of the workings of the real world.

'I'm not criticising or anything, but it's generally best to catch stuff with your hands, not with your face.'

Rapunzel's blood, always on the furiously cool side unless it was boiling with fury, ran then icy-cold *with* hot fury. Rapunzel did a lot of fury. Physical assault followed by mansplaining, eh? she thought. I'm going to use this sucker, get out of this bloody ivory tower and then I'm going to let him know the meaning of the word *pain*. I shall *destroy* him.

At least, she thought, the voice of her thoughts wasn't affected by her *probably* broken nose.

She smiled at Dave – as best she could under the mascara runs and the blood. 'Oh, I'm such a *girl* when it comes to throwing and catching and stuff like that. All my fault. Look – I'm trapped here in this tower. An evil sorceress cast a spell on me.'

'Looks more as though you fell foul of an evil architect, if you ask me' said Dave, having been told that all was well with his new chum, and assuming – innocently - that it really was so. Dave was that unfortunate type of bloke (id est *all* of them) who, if he asked you if there was anything wrong and you replied that there wasn't, believed you. Hashtag #alwaysbelieve. 'Who built this place? Is it a folly of some sort? How did you get up there?'

Rapunzel, smiling, twisted Dave's handkerchief so tightly that the fabric gave a most satisfying little ripping sound. 'The sorceress built it, and she imprisoned me here. She visits me at night-time.'

'Oh' said Dave, his mind wandering between explanations ranging from some sort of domination-based high-altitude lesbian relationship to – no, actually that was all that he could think of with the scant details provided. 'Do you mean she visits at night, stands here and shouts up at you?' he asked, offering Rapunzel a way to side-step the messy sexual mechanics of any arrangement, not wanting to press her on the g-spot, so to speak.

Rapunzel added "really stupid" to her assessment of Dave, although he was, she admitted to herself, built like a brick shit-house and worthy of at least a rumble or two in the old damp duvet machine. He'd probably need a *lot* of training, and she would doubtless have to finish off with Mr Buzzy-Wuzzy, but with standards as high as hers, she thought, that was only to be expected.

'Oh no, she comes up to torture me with expert Italian cooking and superb wines from the fresh and still-vital vineyards of the southern Americas and stuff' explained Rapunzel. 'Thursday night is DVD and pizza and MontGras Antu Cabernet Sauvignon Carmenère night.'

'Oh. Brings a ladder with her?' mused Dave, applying his own early life-experiences of providing a social service to the lonely of the nation to the matter and amending the vocational qualifications of the Sorceress, First Class, to include "Window Cleaner" with a question mark, indicating that as yet he had only supposition, not proof or a bucket or chamois leather or anything by way of evidence.

Rapunzel giggled, regaining her poise and her pose. 'What a twat he is' she thought, as she smiled. 'No, silly! I let down my hair and she climbs up the wall of the tower. I have an awful lot of hair.'

Dave, being a bloke and being practical in such matters, was about to ask Rapunzel whether looking like Cousin It's unkempt Afro-favouring cousin from the neck down saved her anything on heating bills in the winter, but he was interrupted.

Rapunzel threw her long, long, screamingly bright red tresses over the balcony and braced herself expectantly. Well, not *expectantly* yet, but the night was young and condoms have been known to fail if a woman wanted them to. Rapunzel had yet to determine the annual income and average property-holdings and investments of a lumberjack.

'Oh. That's ingenious. Must be exhausting though, and not a little precarious. Brings you your groceries and post the same way too, eh? Wouldn't a ladder be easier?' said Dave.

'No, the Postman brings my post and I've got an order in with the Spar for a home delivery once a week' said Rapunzel. She was getting fed up and wondering whether it might not be easier to go back to waiting again; waiting for something better than Dave to turn up. 'Can we move past this silly practical detail phase please? When the sorceress visits she comes alone, brings nothing and climbs up my hair to get to me.' Rapunzel waggled her hair, trying to give Dave a huge hint. The dandruff released looked like sparkly-sparkly tiny little fairies flying about gaily in the sunlight.

Dave took a step towards the bottom of the tower, where Rapunzel's dazzlingly red locks touched the ground, piling into a heap that, in certain lights, might have been some sort of punk Irish Setter dog lying down and licking its balls. Talking of dogs, Rapunzel's hair had landed in a pile of wolf-poop. Dave decided not to mention it. This was the first sensible thing he'd done since cancelling his weekly Football Pools and putting the entry money into a jam-jar once a week instead.

Chuff-in' finally, thought Rapunzel to herself, seeing him step forwards and peer intently at her hair. Ye gods, how *stupid* are men? She jiggled it about a bit more, and the cloud of wittle faerie-waeries became more dense and more frantic.

Dave, avoiding the icky bits in the wolf poo, picked up the end of Rapunzels train of hair and tested its strength by tugging it between his enormously strong hands.

The penny finally drops, thought Rapunzel, wondering whether she'd made her bed that morning and where the new box of ribbed, pre-lubricated mint-flavoured condoms was. It had been a while since bear-trapper season.

'You've got terrible split ends' said Dave, looking up. 'It's probably because you dye your hair. You'd be better off just touching up the grey rather than dyeing the lot.'

Reaching for his axe Dave promptly began to trim out the split ends (hacking out the wolfy-doo at the same time, hoping that the extra surgery wouldn't be noticed) and then he feathered the whole ensemble, leaving it less heavy, but with more bounce and body.

'I'd add a good proprietary multi-conditioner to your grocery order for next week if I were you.' he said, cheerily.

Rapunzel turned away from the balcony's edge, clenched her hands, claw-fashion, and silently screamed. 'Aaaaaaaaaaaaaarggghhhhh' she thought, before relaxing, putting her smile back on and looking down again.

'Oh thank you, I needed that advice. Men always know these things, don't they? My hair's quite strong, you know, it could easily take your weight.'

'I don't doubt it. It's quite coarse hair really, isn't it? More like dog hair than girl's hair.' Dave immediately regretted mentioning dogs, but it was too late to do more than to discreetly kick aside the pile of off-cuts and the wolf-turds.

Rapunzel harrumphed, but retained her smile. One shag but no more, she thought, just the one – and she wouldn't let him know that she'd enjoyed it even if he made her come like a giddy goose sitting on an ill-secured spin-dryer loaded with house-bricks*.

*An old bear-trapper had done exactly that to Rapunzel some years previously and, although she had thought the twin cassette tape recording machine to be at the pervy end of kinky at the time, she had accepted her copy of the C90 Super-Chrome with Dolby hiss-reduction, and indeed still listened to it often to relieve the long dry spells. Don't judge, we've all been there. Ninety minutes of nostalgia can really lighten the load some days.

'You could easily pull yourself up, you know, if you just tried, and I wouldn't be able to do a thing to stop you once you started. I'm quite defenceless. I couldn't resist you. I'd be totally at your mercy.'

'Aye, that's true enough lass, anyone could pull themselves up. You want to watch yourself, there are some funny buggers in these woodlands. I'd only drop your hair down to folk that you really know, if I were you.'

Might get less wolf and bear shit in it too, thought Dave to himself, quietly.

'I'm absolutely helpless. Don't you want to come up to me?' Rapunzel's breasts actually did then take the plunge as she leant over, popping out of her dress and wedging themselves awkwardly on top of the whale-bone stays, like two blancmanges conversing over a willow hurdle fence. Two happenstances preserved what some might have thought of as her modesty; she was entangled in her own bright red hair and had to fight her way through it for both air and daylight, and when she had done so, Dave was walking back towards the tree-line.

Over his shoulder he called 'Time's getting on and there's work to be done lass. I'll call again tomorrow if I get the chance – maybe bring you a bottle of conditioner for those split ends.'

Rapunzel, briefly beyond words and anxious to do someone violence, wrapped Dave's then-soiled handkerchief around the rock he'd thrown up – and she threw it with all of her might at the back of his head.

She found it infuriating that even with her best throw it still only landed at the base of the tower, on top of what appeared to be either a sleeping Red Setter dog licking its own balls, or a pile of Feminist-Red hair off-cuts garnished with bear shit.

As Dave jogged deeper into the trees he heard that animal screeching sound again, and if he'd been less of a down-to-earth sensible type he could have sworn that

66

whatever animal it was that was in such pain, it had screeched 'FUUUUUUUUCK ME! WAAAAAAAANKER! WHY, WITH ALL THE MEN IN THE WORLD, DO I ONLY EVER MEET THE WANKERS? YE GODS, SEND ME A PUA NOT A MGTOW!' It was very rude, and he hoped that Rapunzel hadn't heard it, whatever it meant.

Dave puzzled all of that afternoon, all of the night and some of the next morning over Rapunzel. He could think of little else, and was quite off his food, toasting only two loaves for breakfast and using just the one 500g jar of Marmite. She must have a reason for staying there. Was she really in a luscious-lesbian lunch-box relationship with a window-washing wine-swilling witch? It seemed probable on the evidence, with the Sorceress possessing a ladder and yet Rapunzel declining to climb down from the tower. As he walked through the woods he kept muttering to himself 'There's nowt so queer as folk, aye, there's nowt so queer as folk.'

Dave wasn't *judging*, you understand. Dave had himself walked on the wild side once in a while. Winters were long and could be lonely in the Big Rutland Forest. Summers weren't so short either, and spring and autumn took their own sweet time to pass too. Why, there had been this one old bear-trapper who – Dave stopped his thoughts and patted a secret pocket in his jacket, making sure that the C90 cassette tape was still safe and sound.

Puzzled or not, Dave was as good as his word, and between felling acres of forest and chopping and stacking wood sufficient unto three HGVs, he took time out to call at his favourite corner shop and to select a bottle of Dandruff-Away with Real Dwarf-Snot Perma-Shine Restorer, a combined shampoo and conditioner suitable for all hair types including lesbian and Feminist. The label advertised the aroma as being a heady mix of unrefined lanolin and coal tar, but the mix was guaranteed to be effective and Rapunzel was on her own in that tower anyway, so it's not as though she was going to mind if her head smelt like a coal-mining sheep-collective. So long as the treatment *worked*, that was the main thing, wasn't it?

Since he was in the bathroom items aisle anyway and was in his usual generous mood he popped a few other things into his basket that Rapunzel, isolated as she was and unable to shop in person, might appreciate. He added box of those sticky strips for pulling out nasal blackheads, two bottles of industrial-strength roll-on deodorant, a bottle of minty-fresh anti-bacterial mouthwash, a box of corn-plasters (one never really knows, does one?), a tin of talcum powder (Lily of the Valley – lovely, does wonders for the lumberjack arse-crack, so it must be good stuff), and a couple of boxes of those heavily-taxed women's products, the ones with wings.

When he reached Rapunzel's tower all was quiet, and at first he feared that she may have gone out or be working in a cellar or the loft something. Then, just as he was about to leave, he heard the toilet cistern cycling and refilling. Rapunzel's voice could be heard, singing the early verses of a folk tune about there being "Cling-ons on the starboard side, starboard side" or some such thing. Rapunzel appeared on the balcony with the words 'scrape 'em off, Jim!'

'Hello' shouted Dave.

Rapunzel squealed and jumped two yards to her left. This was fortunate, since had she jumped two yards to her right the effects of Messrs Gravity (force) and effectively Immovable-Object (the ground) would have been fatally palpable.

'Are you doing The Time Warp?' he asked, with his hands on his hips, pulling his knees in tight and performing a pelvic thrust or two.

'Thuffolk...?' expostulated Rapunzel, being unprepared, and having less than a whole clue.

'No, Rutland. Thuffolk is underneath Northolk, quite near to Ethex. Hello again. I've brought the conditioner for you and a few things I thought you might appreciate, being shopping-challenged, as it were, out here in your tower. I mean, Spar shop deliveries are great, but sometimes the substitutions can be a bit of a pain.'

Rapunzel fumbled with her "home alone" pink plastic NHS coke-bottle bottom spectacles. 'Oh – it's *you*. Changed your mind, have you?'

'I'm here, aren't I? Let down your hair.'

'Maybe I will, and maybe I won't.'

Dave didn't question that the choice was hers. 'As you say, but we won't get far if you don't.'

He found himself awash under a sea of bright-red hair – hair with that faint musty smell that probably meant someone wasn't spending enough time drying it out thoroughly after bath-time. Not surprising really though; it would take more than six-hundred watts of Pifco with inflatable hood attachment to dry this lot properly.

'OK, pull' he cried.

Rapunzel, putting her heart and soul into it and stepping back on the balcony as she tugged was surprised by her own strength. Mr Built-Like-A-Brick-Shit-House was as light as a feather.

I AM WOMAN! SEE ME PULL! She said to herself at the top of her voice, deciding that she must have the strength of ten men at least. If you want to hoist a two-hundred and fifty pound he-man up the side of a fifty-foot high tower then get a woman to do it. Perhaps, she thought, men were lighter once all of their blood had rushed out of their little brains and into their little penises?

It was a spot of a disappointment therefore when after much theatrical huffing and puffing and laying out of her hair as though it were a skein of wool, a plastic bag from the Spar Shop plopped over the parapet and hit the stone flags. A box of blackhead plasters, mouthwash and a box of incontinence pads rolled out (all heavily-taxed feminine hygiene products with wings look the same to all men – we have neither clue nor, TBH, care).

Dave, fifty feet below, heard that "animal in extreme pain" sound again and he wondered what the hell had happened. Rapunzel did seem to be awfully accident-prone. Somehow, whatever had befallen Rapunzel this time involved a tin of talcum powder missing Dave's head by inches. He sniffed – Lily of The Valley. Lovely. Just the thing for lumberjack crack.

'What's up? Is it the wrong sort?' asked Dave, looking up at a thunder cloud that had formed at the top of the tower, and was beginning to crackle with lightning bolts.

A large bottle of deodorant hit a mossy rock near where he was standing, and shattered. Well, at least that rock won't have a problem any time soon with unsightly under-arm patches, he thought. Dave was hard-wired to always look on the bright side of life.

'YOU BASTARD!' shrieked Rapunzel. 'ALL MEN ARE BASTARDS! WHY DOES NOBODY UNDERSTAND ME?'

Dave backed away slowly. 'Sorry, I did my best. Why don't we both go to the Spar Shop now, and you can choose your own stuff, eh? I'll carry it all back here for you.' Being nice and helpful was *such* a minefield!

The second bottle of deodorant whizzed past not ten yards from his left ear. Rapunzel's throwing was improving – at about £2.49 a shot not including Corner Shop Loyalty Points.

'HOW MANY TIMES MUST I EXPLAIN THAT I AM TRAPPED HERE? THE SORCERESS IMPRISONED ME HERE!'

Dave dithered a little and he hesitated. He knew that it wasn't going to end well but something in him, something of the spirit of the Black & Decker, something of his legacy as a man who could bang nails in straight every time he picked up a hammer forced its way to his mouth and left his body.

'Why don't you use your hair to escape then? Just tie it to something and climb down...'

Being hit full in the knackers by a preternaturally well-thrown bottle of anti-dandruff shampoo was all the hint that Dave needed. He retreated, taking the shampoo with him (waste not want not). Rapunzel had indeed mastered the art of throwing things.

With the exception of the bottle of shampoo squarely into Dave's todging-tackle, the main thing that Rapunzel threw well that afternoon was a tantrum.

Nobody, but nobody, not one single, stupid man, seemed prepared to help a girl in distress. All he would have had to do would be to climb up a fifty-foot tall stone tower using her hair, ravish her brains out as his *ample* reward, and then sling her over his sage-green English tweed gilet-covered, very, very muscular shoulder* and carry her down to freedom whereupon she would scream, call the police, allege some serious sexual assault and claim her compensation money. Simples, but no, he just wasn't capable.

*We've established earlier in this tale that *both* of Dave's shoulders were muscular, so stop that.

Well, there was nothing else for it. She would have to rescue herself. What was it he'd said? Just before 'OUCH! Right in me bollocks, feck me that *really really* hurt!'? Rapunzel wracked her brain. Oh yes – he'd said 'tie your hair to something'. Well, to be brutally honest and not meaning to offend anyone's feelings, if a chuffing *man* could do it then Rapunzel was sure that she could too – and do it in high heels.

She carefully wound her hair a couple of times around the cat and knotted the end in a pretty bow.

Then she walked out onto the balcony and climbed over the parapet, expecting to be able to walk *down* the outside of the tower perpendicular to the stonework and looking as cool as a cucumber in a picnic saandwich.

Mr Snuggles *just* had time to look slightly unconvinced by the mechanics of the arrangement.

'AAAAAAAAAAAAAAAAARRRRRRRRRRRRRGG GGGGGGGGGGGGGHHHHH!'

BASTARD MEN! He'd given her the wrong instructions.

Mr Snuggles, doing the best that he could to resist forces far beyond any domestic cat's realistic purview, left scratch marks clean across the tower floor. Spreading-eagling himself as only a cat can he briefly, very briefly, arrested their motion at the balcony door-frame, lost the battle and flew out into the open air with a wailing cry to rival that of Rapunzel herself.

Rapunzel was wailing because she could see the ground rocketing up to meet her. This had never been part of her plan, she'd wanted a slow and controlled descent followed by a gentle tug on her hair and for Mr Snuggles to fall pleasingly – and pleased with both of themselves – into her arms.

'FUUUUUUUUUUUUUCK PHYSICS!' she cried on the way down.

'A PLAGUE UPON YOUR DAMNED STEM SUBJECTS!' she shrieked.

'BASTAAAAAARD PATRIARCHYYYYY!'

There then followed two thuds, one of them much more significant in terms of Rapunzel's existential continuation vis-a-vis the Land of The Living than the other.

Rapunzel's never-ever-try-this-at-home-children "thud" had a sort of "broken spine/fractured skull" motif about it.

Mr Snuggles' thud was, as cats' thuds are oft wont to be, more like four paws landing on the ground, followed by a "Christ on a pogo stick, that was legendary and I'll bet not one bastard other cat actually saw it" meow, somewhere on the plaintive side of C-sharp. Mr Snuggles sat on his haunches and took a *very* casual swift wash of himself, one back leg in the air.

Mind you, would Mr Snuggles have wanted to have been seen, with fifty feet of Feminist-red riah wrapped around his waist? The point is moot.

As night fell and temperatures dipped Mr Snuggles found his way over towards his beloved mistress's body (where there was at least some residual warmth to be had, her ruptured vitals cooling less swiftly than her ruptured less-than-vitals).

Later, much later, when the Sorceress came for her customary night-time visit, Mr Snuggles had re-arranged himself so that he looked like a cat's head poking out from a tangled mass of blood-red angel-hair spaghetti. He purred a greeting and then meowed a summary of pertinent recent events. Purrrrrr-tinent recent events. Apparently he hadn't been fed and he really, really needed to use his litter tray but couldn't extricate himself from the hair of his former keeper and it smelt as though there was a bear or a wolf nearby and would the new madam please assist with all possible dispatch on all ppppoints prrrrrrrreviously mentioned?

The sorceress put down her bucket and chamois leather, and propped her ladder against the tower wall.

'Buggeration!' she said. 'Whatever do they teach these girls at school?'

The part-time sorceress full-time window cleaner looked down at Mr Snuggles. 'I blame the rise of single parent families and the court system's almost unfailing preference for awarding custody to the mother, however unsuitable. A father-figure in her life would surely have taught the poor girl that a domestic cat is a wholly unsuitable animal to tether oneself to before any sort of flying farking follicular fifty-foot fling.'

Mr Snuggles agreed, and immediately transferred his full affections, allegiances and favourite fleas.

The Sorceress used her cold, wet chamois-leather to remove the make-up from Rapunzel's face (make-up now much in disarray) and then walked up the side of the tower, dragging Rapunzel by the ankle.

Rapunzel was in some disarray. She had so many broken bones that she was more like a maraca than a human. The sorceress took a few rumba steps over to the First Aid kit and retrieved the Dettol. Also the Deep Heat, the Deep Cold, two waterproof sticking plasters (the big ones that you only get two of in any multi-pack in spite of their being the most useful of all sizes) and a tub of Andrews Liver Salts. Emptying them all over Rapunzel's life-free body the sorceress intoned the magic words.

'N.H.S., N.H.S., I've paid National Insurance Contributions for my whole miserable working life, I'm in the N.H.S. Our Health Minister, who art at his second home in Devon, hallowed be thy name. Heal the bitch, heal the bitch, you have to do this because I'm a witch.'

Rapunzel's body began to twitch violently, and the sorceress knew then just where the inspiration had come from for John Hurt's losing battle with Sigourney Weaver's alien.

Skipping in circles the sorceress continued the spell. 'Oh, the leg bone's connected to the... head bone. The head bone's connected to the... bum bone. The spine bone's connected to the... knee-bone. Hear the word of the Lord.'

Rapunzel's eyes opened, and she gurgled up a bit of blood and bile.

'Shush little baby, don't you cry – big sister's going to make it all better.'

For her own safety, the Sorceress then took the shears to Rapunzel's hair and left her instead with a nice, tidy, easy-to-manage, bright red, Number 2 crop.

The sorceress leaned in closely to hear Rapunzel's weak whisper. 'Shall I... shall I make a full recovery? I shall make a full recovery, shan't I?'

The sorceress smiled.

'No dear, you're going to look like something that fell out of a fifty-foot tower onto hard rocks below for the rest of your life, but don't worry – I'll make Tiramisu for Thursday's pudding, and we can watch Thelma & Louise again – *all* night if you like.'

Mr Snuggles, declining to remain longer in the tower, walked back down the stonework alongside the sorceress, following her home and moving in, settling on a pile of child-peelings next to her bubbling cauldron.

To this very day Rapunzel still lives in the tower, a little bit bent-over because of the broken spine that had never been treated professionally and with a head shaped like a deflated medicine-ball because of the fractured skull, wishing that she still had a cat (or twelve), and hating all men with a visceral hate known only unto Feminism. She keeps herself busy weaving her old long hair into material that is as strong as steel and as light as a feather, and some day, some day very soon, she's going to sew it into a parachute and escape that tower for once and for all.

Once in a while, as Dave's work takes him close to the tower in the glade in the valley in the less-frequently visited part of Big Rutland Forest, he fancies that he can hear someone shouting 'I HATE SODDING THELMA AND SODDING LOUISE!'

Dave always shouts back, as loudly as he can – which is *very* loudly indeed – 'BUGGER ME, DARLING, DON'T WE ALL!'

Anyway.

Dave found the gnarled and knotted tree that he was looking for and made his old mother a lovely new dining table. There was so much wood left over that he was also able to make himself a billiards table and a card table, both of which he and his lumberjack friends enjoyed on a regular basis (being careful to put their beer cans down only on the coasters provided).

Sleeping Beauty

Single Ford Transit Mk1 vans were not often seen entering the Big Mysterious Old Woods near Grimsby. *Convoys* of such vans, laden with pickaxes and sledgehammers and cement mixers and hairy-arsed builders were even more rare.

One such convoy threaded its way gingerly through the massive wrought-iron entrance gates of the Big Mysterious Old Woods estate, intent on finding and negotiating the driveway, somehow. After several rather sporting attempts by drivers Bill, Will and Gazza, attempts that ended in much wheel-spin and derisive laughter, a way was found; the builders alighted from their vehicles and went ahead with machetes and chainsaws and flame-throwers.

Had this been Africa and not England, Doctor Livingstone would likely have approved.

After several unscheduled days of delay the convoy of envoys of Messrs Noguar & Teae, Builders of Distinction, found their way into the heart of the darkness, and, by dint of some cunning following of the arrow signs erected to assist visitors, to the castle that inevitably lies at the heart of every big, mysterious old woods.

Messrs Noguar & Teae had been retained by the executors to find Worthabobortwo Castle, and then to raze it to the ground and to prepare the land for a lucrative new ticky-tacky "affordable" housing development to encourage young buyers into the heavy chains that are the world of mortgages and property taxes and unavoidable business relationships with huge and international "utility supply" corporations. Um, I mean of course *onto the bottom rung of the housing market*. Yes, yes, that's what I mean. Not slavery at all, no chains involved, tis but freely and eagerly "investing in the future".

Investing their souls with Messrs Beelzebub PLC.

Anyway. The first stage of any *"diverse development plan that will bring homes and jobs and prosperity to the neighbourhood and a brand spanking new Austin Montego 1.6LX to the personal driveways of most of the council members on rather favourable no deposit no payment we'll forget we leased it to you terms"* is to send in the disposable apes.

Men.

Bugger, did I just type that out loud? To send in the *workmen*. Workmen, skilled workmen, highly valued by society, yes, that's it. The first stage of any carefully considered eco-friendly long-term social-investment for your children's future (the future of those members of the Council already being secure), is to send in the hairy-arsed builders to knock stuff down wiv a 'ammer.

The old driveway leading to Worthabobortwo Castle was long and twisting, and it led past several sizeable lakes, a delightful folly and a private cemetery choc-full of unfashionably deceased dead people, all pinned down under sizeable slabs of marble. When the robber-baron ruling classes play a game of marbles, they *really* play a game of marbles.

The gravestones all had dates and a little bit of history carved into them.

'Here lies King Thingummy-Wotsit. Gone but not forgiven.'

'In Loving Memory of The Queen. Taken from us during the Great Plague (killed in a duel).'

'Some Dead Prince or Other. He pushed his luck too far, and was twatted by The King.'

'Dulce Et Decorum Est Pro Patria Mori. Princess, The People's, One, Well-Deceased. Blah-Blah-Blah. It is what as I had her done in because it was that the people did like her more than me, and I'm Queen, innit.'

The castle itself was your standard minor robber-baron nouveau-gothic affair, with drawbridge, six-point deadlock portcullis, five towers, four reception rooms, ample machicolations to all points of the compass, and eight bedrooms all with en-suite drop-through privy-chamber feeding into the common moat. There was a Great Hall, a Not-So-Great Hall, one Solar, two Chapels and an Inside Dovecote with separate Plucking Room. There was a Casemate, a reasonably roomy Place of Arms, three Undercrofts and a suite of cellars including stretching rack rooms, screaming chambers and an "Ooh eck – I'd quite forgotten we'd chained *him* up, better just bury him quietly somewhere" room.

From a builder's bum view it was just a shame that no-one had done any maintenance for several centuries (none at all since the Mk 1 Queen Elizabeth came out of the factory, really, and *that* model didn't even have wheels).

The Noguar & Teae Site Foreman, Bert, held his chin in that foreman-ish way and he just knew at once that the wiring would be dodgy, very dodgy indeed. The trick with medieval electrical wiring, you see, is to keep the wooden insulation well-varnished, and it was surely certain that a ten-litre tin of shellac hadn't been opened on this site since Boudicca was knee-high to her hockey mistress.

Bert personally supervised the unloading and erection of the site's Health & Safety Greeting board, the one with the advice and little symbols about hard-hats and hi-vis underwear and steel-capped nipple-guards and about not eating nuts and bolts and about never ever attempting to start large diesel generators with your penis even if there is significant money on the table and you're so pissed that you're certain that you can do it.

The vast and hugely solid oak doors of Worthabobortwo Castle were locked. Bert gave the handles a good rattle just to make sure, and then he turned and told Derek to 'run a bypass'.

Derek, whom everyone usually assumed just happened to walk with a limp, extracted a metre-long crowbar from a special pocket in his work trousers, and he bypassed the locking mechanism. Derek occasionally came in for some light-hearted peer-group criticism about his being firmly located at the lower end of the Male line of the Variability IQ Curve, but nobody ever questioned his ability to kick down a door, any door. I mean, to "run a bypass". Never. Not once. Derek re-inserted the crowbar into his trousers and re-adopted his limp. The doors fell off their hinges and began the tedious prospect of awaiting the architectural reclamation van.

Several woodworm and four small Deathwatch Beatles scuttled away.

Bert gave the rather predictable quotable quote always quoted before the team embarked on any job where Derek's skills had been called upon.

'You're only supposed to blow the bloody Doors off.'

Derek, as we've already intimated, being not the brightest little bulb to fall off the Christmas Tree, looked puzzled. 'Thazzall I did, Boss... Just the doors, you said, just the doors I done did.'

The team quietly reassured Derek that everything was fine. No worries. Gotcha covered.

Once the dust of The Ages had settled a little the team advanced.

Time had not been kind.

Worthabobortwo Castle was a shit-hole.

There were bold geometric-patterned wallpapers everywhere, any surface that wasn't Formica was covered in Fablon, and the linoleum on the floors throughout was cracked and worn and hinted at the sort of interior decorators who hold court in television home-makeover shows and who are working to a budget of two farthings per room.

Bert gasped. 'Stand back, lads – I'm going in. Tell my wife I love her very much and that the life insurance policy is in my sock drawer under my back-editions of Bikini Nun Pictorial.'

'Nice one, Bert!'

'I thought so. Hidden where she would never look, thus reducing the chances of my being murdered for the insurance money. My Dad taught me a thing or two. Grand-dad taught him. It's the kind of thing that males of the family do for one another; how to ride a bike, first pint, how to handle your first kiss, how to not get killed for the insurance money.'

As Bert advanced into the various wipe-clean vinyl wallpapers of the retreating years so his gang of men advanced bravely at not some little distance behind him. Neville held his sledgehammer as might a mountain dwarf entering the House of Commons. Wayne carried the business end of his pneumatic drill over his shoulder as though it were a missile launcher. Albert, whose chief duties generally lay in providing hot tea and Hobnobs, had his huge tea-strainer in one hand and the team's stirring spade in the other. Goodness me, but they were a terrifying sight. If trouble presented itself then Neville could hammer it on the head, Wayne could drill it in the throat, and Albert could spoon it in the goolies.

Even the old suits of armour were wise enough to remain on their podiums. Podiuii. Podii. Whatever; they remained quiet and out of the way.

Bert communicated silently with military hand-gestures, indicating "fan out, lads, and watch your backs" and "oh - watch your spacing too – I've just farted".

They separated and explored, coughing a little but not from the dust.

From a bedroom on the first floor Oz screamed, the horses bits, had there been any, would have been covered in foam, and the hens, had there been any of those about, would have hitched up their skirts and run pell-mell back into their sheds. The lads all converged on Oz's position by a process of clever triangulation (Albert was also in the works' orchestra and carried his instrument at all times, including the little "dinger"). Oz was found in the corridor outside the bedroom, breathing hard and looking pale.

'Wazzup?'

Oz's eyes were somehow disconnected from reality. Bert administered a supervisory poke in the chest with a bony finger. Oz recovered faster than a Twitter-trauma victim upon discovering the efficacy of non-microscopic frontal-lobes and the "easy report and block" function.

'Woman. In there. Dead. A right munter.'

Bert pressed for detail. 'Blood?'

'No thanks, I'd rather have tea. Tea's better for shock' replied Oz.

Albert nodded and passed forward his emergency flask with the top already loosened. The top could be a sod at times, and he liked to loosen it before prescribing oral infusions.

'Can't be doing with blood. Blood and guts and mess' said Bert. 'I'm a married man, I've seen too much of that since the vicar said 'I now denounce you man and wife.'

Bert decided that *someone* had to venture back into the room on a quasi-scientific, fact-finding mission to obtain sufficient verifiable and empirical data on which to formulate a reasonable and efficacious finite sequence of necessarily reactive but nonetheless adaptive future events designed to facilitate the completion of their assigned commercial task without further undue delay or complication while also maintaining human dignity, following local end-of-life customs, achieving a safe, secure and stress-limited working environment for his men, and getting the stiff carted away into the care of the authorities before the smell got any worse.

He pushed Wayne through the door.

'Bert?' called Wayne, after a short yelp of volunterring-surprise followed by a long coughing fit of most tentative exploration.

'Yes, Wayne?' said Bert, anxious as ever to provide a light-house rock of support upon which his colleagues may allow their various seas of personal and professional troubles to crash.

'You can come in, Bert, you'll be fine, it's just dust and cobwebs and spiders and mould and mildew and mouse-droppings. Decor's a bit Miss Havisham. There's no obvious blood. You can all come in.'

Sure enough, there was a right mun... an unfortunate woman in the room. Legs akimbo, shoes kicked off to the floor to land among the empty White Lightning bottles and the puddles of ancient, long-dried vomit, she seemed to have only just made it to the four-poster bed before passing out. She was dressed in a short, red, strapless number and, in terms of her make-up and hairstyle, appeared to have pushed her head in and out of a cow's rectum several times before hitting the pillow. There was a curry take-away on the bedside table, still in its white plastic bag, untouched.

They all removed their hard-hats and lowered their heads respectfully for a moment.

Then they all turned to Bert. 'Shouldn't someone say something, you know, a few words of introduction to the various Misters God that she might have gone to meet, that sort of thing?' said the gestalt. 'We commend this soul, Lords various Almighty, blah blah bollocks, let her into whichever Heaven she believes in and give her a nice room with a view of the duck pond?'

Bert began to open his mouth to speak.

The woman made a noise like a Gloucester Old Spot gagging on a bucketful of cold brawn.

Being married, Bert recognised the exact sound. 'Jebus H – she's snoring!'

Everyone in the little semi-circle jumped back. It was as though they were suddenly engaged in some brief but highly energetic version of the hokey-cokey, the bit where you put your whole self *out*.

'There's a note pinned to her dress' observed Bert. 'Get it, Derek. We'll have to read it.'

'Norfolk'n'chance' replied Derek. 'If you think I'm fiddling around with the clothing of some passed-out woman you've got another think coming.'

Being builders, they came up with a technological solution. While Derek resisted vis-a-vis counter-weighting, Albert, always pragmatic, extended the claw of his "litter picker" towards the note and drew it away.

The note was written on lined notepaper torn from some sort of spiral-bound pad, possibly a medieval shorthand-notebook discarded by some secretary of the castle. It was written in green Biro, the sort that blotches every once in a while because there's a lumpy bit of ink stuck to the ballpoint, the sort of blotch that *never* seems to wipe off no matter how many times you try a few side-swipes in the margin. These margins were themselves highly and densely decorated with intricate knot-work scrolls and with zoomorphic illustrations which, thought Bert, spoke wordlessly of adoption and adaptation from the later periods of the Germanic style, thus accurately dating the note to somewhere between "who knows" and "might have been last week for all Bert knew".

Bert screwed in his "foreman builder's monocle", squinted and read the note aloud.

'I has curs-ed this woeman unto a vewy vewy deep sleep on account of some wrongs what was done to me by her parents. She can only be WOKE by the kiss of a faery prince. No fakes, mind you, he must be da real fing and da kiss mun be on da lips full and true, with a little tung and lots of that "nom nom nom" sound like two randy teenagers trying to eat each other's face off. XOXOXO, Hilda, your friendly neighbourhood Sorceress. Grudges two a groat, flayings sixpence plus VAT.'

Bert saw it at once. The whole plot. The reference to immature teenagers helped. 'I see it at once' he said. 'The whole plot. Two households, both alike in dignity, in fair Verona, where we lay our scene. One unconscious, one uneducated. From ancient grudge break to new mutiny, where civil blood makes civil hands unclean.'

'Huh?' came the chorus of reply, in the sort of tones that indicated "look, you may be the foreman but if you're getting hoity-toity on us again with the book-learning stuff then you're in for a twatting".

'Issa tragedy, innit. Poor lass, cursed and as good as dead forever.'

'No she in't. We've *got* a prince.' Neville, who was as fond of advancing others in their careers as was Bert, pushed Harry, the young apprentice paint-stirrer and spirit-level-bubble fetcher forward. 'Harry's a prince among men.'

'*And* he's a fairy' added Wayne. 'Makes 'im a fairy-prince, dunnit.'

Young Harry blushed and kicked at the carpet. Being several centuries old and having been subject to damp and to cursed-lady vomit, the carpet ripped and shrank back into itself. Dust flew and the spiders of ages past scattered and retreated into corners and under the bed and up the walls. Several of them were caught in one another's webs, to be eaten later, but such is the circle of life.

'Go on, Harry – give 'er a kiss. Nom nom nom nom nom.'

'Can't.' replied Harry, fiddling with his stirring-stick and releasing a replacement spirit-level bubble from his secret, trouser-based store of such things, his asymmetric haircut falling over his face and hiding him from view, much to his relief. 'T'ain't right.' He tugged his "I would be What A Feminist Looks Like but Mummy says I'm still busy being her Special Little Snowflake" t-shirt into folds, and he scratched at a (pierced) nipple (one of his own).

'Whyzat? She's a girl [the assessment was generous, to the tune of some thirty or forty years apparent, and several centuries actual] and you're a boy. S'only pullin' yer leg when we calls you a fairy' said Dillon, part of the team, but one who never seemed to be at the forefront of things or to be entirely memorable. Dillon twanged his acoustic guitar and went back to looking spaced-out.

'Snot that' said Harry. 'Tud be sexual assault. She can't give no constant and enthusiastic consent for me to do sex on 'er. She be got herself the worse for drink and thus her safety now be the 'sponsibility of every man on the planet what do now have a duty of care and mun change *their* lives to accommodate the mistakes the Patriarchy has forced her to make in hers.'

'Curse, lad, she be the worse for *curse*, not drink' said Bert, stubbing his toe on an empty crate previously used to hold White Lightning bottles. 'Although from the evidence, drink may have played a part in things. Tis different with a curse, if she don't get kissed she mun as well be dead. You be killin' 'er by *not* kissin' 'er. Tis a fate almost as bad as death is being killed by not bein' kissed, it is. Judge'd go lightly on 'ee. Stenuatin' circumstances.'

'Don't make no matter' replied Harry, sticking to his gun, and sticking a little to his poorly-maintained and slightly sticky paint-stirring stick. He found the situation excruciating. He hadn't been this excruciated for at least ten minutes.

'Kid's right' said Wayne. 'It's... *The Law*. Constant and enthusiastic consent swots needed.'

'Wozza consent swot when it's at home?'

'Like a PostIt, innit, but she 'as to write lots of 'em. Kiss me, kiss me, kiss me, now roger me senseless big boy, harder, harder, harder, faster, faster, faster, gently, gently, gently, slowly, slowly, slowly, oh god, oh god, OH GOD,

CHRIST ALMIGHTY AND ALL OF THE APOSTLES
ON ELECTRIC POGO STICKS, pfft! that it? wish that had
been as good for me as it obviously was for you, you
bastard, now get off me I've changed my mind and I'm
going to press charges – that sort of thing. Paper trail,
f'revidence in court.'

'Tis silly! T'would be *medical* kiss. Here, I'll do it. I'm
old enough to be her father' opined Bert, the most
unreconstructed of all of them due to his propensity for
whippets and pigeons and the Sunday tabloids.

In actual fact, the sleeping beauty was old enough to be
Bert's great-to-the-Nth-grandmother, so no-one there
present could work out who, on the evidence of a medicinal
kiss, would actually be the paedophile of the two.

'That's even worse' said Wayne, gently stopping Bert in
his tracks, as you do if you're the caring sort of chap and
the Foreman is about to stumble into a world of crucifixion-
by-changed-mind-and-bonker's-regret-framed-as-heinous-
assault-post-facto.

'How?'

'Makes you a dirty old man in the eyes of the law.'

'S'true. Forget the Unemployment Office; you'd have to
sign on at the Sex Registry for life.'

'AND the other inmates would cut your balls off –
virtue signalling. White Knights love cutting other bloke's
balls off.'

'Well what if we got a *woman* to kiss her? A woman
who self-identified as a prince.'

'Hmm. Might work. What we would need is a *thespian*
with royal aspirations.'

'Now *there's* an idea that has legs.'

'Lots of thespians have legs.'

'Makes you wonder what they use 'em all for.'

They all drifted off into a moment's philosophical
contemplation of the purpose of thespian legs, and then
someone had a bright idea.

'Dave's sister's that way inclined – at least, I think she must be - she wouldn't kiss me on New Year's Eve. Only explanation is she's a thespian. Nice legs too.'

'*Everyone* wouldn't kiss you on New Year's Eve. Anyway, doesn't count. Not since the case of von Dieseltitz versus Goldilox, 2016' said Harry, who since puberty had always kept such legal notices Sellotaped up on the ceiling above his bunk bed, in the space where former generations kept centrefolds of Pamela Anderson and/or Diana Dors (the most popular poster among boys of a certain age being the one of the two of them together, in the sunlight, wading out of the Humber Estuary at the Cleethorpes foreshore).

'Note says a prince, anyway. It's in the text of the curse, and prince means a *man*.'

'Not necessarily. What if we found a thespian who *self-identified* as a prince?'

'No good – he married a domifemininistrix, renounced the title and moved to Canada and then Canada made them move on to Los Angeles.' A second shocked hush fell upon the company as they remembered the newscasts of early twenty-twenty in re the unfortunate Sussex royal who had surrendered his royal balls without a single shot being fired.

'Anyway, still falls, under the judgement of Dickinson versus Dickindaughter, 2014, or some such precedent. Assault whoever does it or to whomever it's done.'

'Precedent's no good – 'as to be a prince' said one whose grasp of the robber-baron hierarchy honorific structure was loose at best.

'You mean that unless she's constantly mumbling into a tape recorder "oh god, oh please, yes YEEE-ESSS, big boy, as a strong and empowered female I do hereby consent and wholly agree without *duress* but *with* Durex to having big sex done upon me by your faery princeness at xx o'clock on dd/mm/yy" as the prince give her a peck on the lips to release her from the curse it's...'

'Yep. Boundaries.'

'Personal autonomy.'

'A woman's right to choose.'

'Choose what?'

'Everything.'

'Oh.'

'Kiss her now and tomorrow morning she'd wake up with pillow-face and change her mind and call the police. If you got rich in twenty years time she'd have you in court faster than you could say do excuse me, but &etc. You'd be forced to be a film director or a producer or something. Tudbe gaol fer life.'

'What about a ventriloquist. Someone could move her lips. Gottle of gear. Give me that curse-breaking kiss, big goy...'

They all agreed that "big goy" was very reverse-un-anti-non-semitic, and as such, unacceptable no matter the quality of or the good intentions of the ventriloquist.

They all scratched their brains for a while in desperation, and we all know that workmen's brains are, by law, located either side of the valley running through the Builder's Bum mountains.

'What about the dog? If we named the dog Prince... he already thinks he's royalty...'

Now that, they all agreed, was an idea that had also legs, even if it wasn't a lesbian. Four of them in fact. Five if you followed his tracks through snow or loose sand. They all hunted around for the Official Building-Site Dog, and found him enthusiastically shitting in a corner of the Great Hall. Bert did the honours.

'Mister Dog, I rename thee Prince. Now get in there and kiss the bride.'

Mister Do... *Prince* was picked up and held face to face with the sleeping beauty. Try as they might, Prince turned his head away from the face more inventively than they could hold him at that awkward angle (it was the worst case of vomit-lips he'd seen in years, and that was saying something, given that Prince was a dog and therefore not averse to eating his own vomit).

Once they put him down again of course he was quite happy to hump her leg. Her leg was relatively vomit-free, and had an intriguing texture about it, being as hairy as a slightly-balding teddy-bear.

'Curses, failed again, if you'll pardon my paraphraseologyism' said Bert. 'I'm out of ideas. We'll have to call in the professionals.'

Wayne got out his autograph book and went to the bedroom window to watch for a Ford Escort MkII RS2000 and a Ford Capri 3.0 S MkIII to slew to a halt on the gravel outside.

Bert used his work's mobile to dial 999, first entering his PIN and then having to re-dial several times because the "keyboard" was far too tiny for adult human *male* fingers to use with any accuracy, the devices being designed for the use of women, children and neurosurgeons working at the dainty end of the neurosurgery market.

Beep beep beep beep boop barp boop beep beep beep beep boop bong barp borp baap boop beep beep boop beep beep beep beep beep beep beep beep beep beep boop bong barp borp baap boop beep beep boop beep beep beep beep beep beep beep.

'Hello? Police please. We've found a young lady who is unconscious, cursed by a sorceress. Location? Worthabobortwo Castle. Which three what? Words? Oh. What three words. An "app" you say? Hang on while I check... [beep beep beep boop bong barp borp baap boop beep beep boop beep beep beep beep beep beep beep beep beep beep boop bong barp borp baap boop beep beep boop beep beep beep beep beep beep beep beep beep boop bong barp borp baap boop beep beep boop beep beep beep beep beep beep beep beep beep beep boop bong barp borp baap boop beep beep boop beep beep beep beep beep beep beep beep beep beep boop bong barp borp baap boop beep

beep boop beep beep beep beep beep beep beep beep] The Wot Free Words app says ///Sexual.Assault.Obviously. Oh. Map reference? Oh – um – er – beep, beep beep - 53.807139 1.4996338. Country? England. It's quite near Europe but not actually *in* it. Planet? Oh – third one out from the sun, Sol, we call it 'Earth'. Huh? Oh, about a dozen blokes. No, no women present other than the one who is passed out. What? Oh – thank you. Yes, we'll be here. We'll put the kettle on. What? Why? Oh, alright, fine, fine... oh.'

The phone's battery died.

The call centre operator for the English police, a gentleman called 'Melanie' and who was sitting in Bombay in India, spoke into his headset to the Home Secretary.

'No sir, I had control of the mobile telephone and pictures were coming through but then the battery died. No sir, I cannot recharge it by remote control, I wish that I could. That technology is not yet widely available to me. You must ask your boss to send police men most urgently, this poor woman is unsupervised and is in exclusively male company. Thank you. Hit them like one of your proverbial tons of bricks. Arrive with all possible dispatch and you will take them by surprise, although I have told them that you are coming.'

Yardley-Gobb, the *Shadow* Home Secretary, had given up explaining to the call centre staff that she wasn't *that* sort of secretary, but something much, much more important, almost a boss in her own right, and she took notes to pass on to the Chief Constable's secretary. It was just easier to answer to "sir" and to take messages and pass them on than to keep explaining that a Home Secretary was actually a Very Important Woman. Person, a Very Important Person-Woman. Besides, she quite liked it when her little mobile phone rang, and it kept her busy and out of mischief. Plus, by keeping her hand in at *real* secretarial duties she kept herself more employable, a sort of Plan B for should she ever somehow tragically lose the undying respect of her electorate and/or the party faithful.

Bert considered the proper ball to be rolling.

'Police are on their way. I think. 999 gets you to some sort of foreign call-centre these days. The chap – said his name was Melanie – Bombay accent by the sound of him - said that we all had to wait here and touch nothing as it would all be needed for evidence and would definitely be used against us later in court. Asked me to peer at my phone as though I were having a passport photo taken and then the battery died.'

'Is it actually possible to touch nothing, existentially speaking?'

'No, but you *can* get a conviction in court these days on the basis of nothing at all – even untouched nothing and very little of it.'

'What court?'

'Well, this one, I suppose – it was all royal courts and stuff in the days of shights in kniming armour, wasn't it. You know, when women were ladies not Feminists and men were gentlemen and jousted all day every day to win their hearts and a bit'o flimsy headscarf, that sort of thing.'

'Sounds like a right silly waste of time and effort if you ask me' said a voice from the fireplace, possible that of Prince. Prince was humping the coal-scuttle.

The sound of police-car sirens grew louder. There was the sound of one of them not managing the turn off from the main road into the driveway and smashing at speed into a stone gatepost, but the others paused not, and they grew closer. Whatever the police code for 'unconscious woman surrounded by gentlemen' was, it obviously elicited an all-out blues & twos response. It's a good bet that the machines guns and police dogs and riot shields were fair bouncing around in the boots of those cars.

A selection of British Leyland's finest then arrayed itself in the courtyard by the front door, white and pale blue Mini

Metro 1.0L cheek by tyre-jowl with white and pale blue Austin Allegro 1.3, white and blue Austin Maxi 1750HL vying for parking space with two white and blue Morris Marinas (*one* a Coupé 1.8TC!). The Chief Constable's sombre burgundy Wolseley Six hove right up to the front door. Two black Leyland Sherpa vans brought up the rear which, when you think about it, was a terrible systemic insult to people of colour, excluding of course from that definition of colour anything *privileged* #FFFFFF to *apoplectic* #FFC0CB, and it was an undeniable vehicular *F U* to our loyal Gurkha friends in Nepal.

Hob-nail boots on hob-nail feet then thundered up the sweeping staircase. Bert thought that he ought to call out some warning about dry rot and "not so much weight all at one time", but there was no time for such niceties. Besides, the English police were used to things collapsing under their feet, things such as high-profile cases for mass and massive child-abuse in South Yorkshire.

In point of fact the ancient staircase didn't collapse, although the charge up it did. There was a grasping of handrails, a leaning of backs up against walls and a sitting down on steps halfway through the constabulary stampede. Legal opinion as they paused, some standing hands on knees, and all gasping for breath, was that there was a right buggering lot of steps in the flight and that a law ought to be passed requiring all crime to be committed on the ground floor.

Eventually, Bert and the lads experienced an unlooked-for juxtaposition and momentum-laden contact each with an eager, re-invigorated (in some cases re-animated) member of the constabulary, an adjustment in personal altitude to floor-level and a cuff-based disconvenience of the forearms, wrists and hands. The constabulary *knee in the kidneys* was pure gravy for most. The air was *thick* with the fumes and vapours of virtue-signalling.

"There's a woman – and you're all just bastard animal men" the beatings said in not so many coherent words. It was a sort of an ideological non-sequitur beating, but with real, not ideological knuckles.

From his position face sideways on and in a patch of dried lady-vomit Bert could see Prince, the dog formerly known as Mr Dog, enjoying the same sort of playful rough-housing before being restrained with not one but two pairs of hand-cuffs, one for his front paws, one for his rear paws. He was quite clearly enjoying a little bit of BDSM, doggy style, and was wagging his tail and trying to lick all eight of the policemen holding him down.

As the dust of centuries began to settle the Chief Constable made her entrance.

'Youuuuuuuu bastards. You'll hang for this. All of you.'

Prince, formerly known as Mr Dog, looked wide-eyed at Authority Incarnate, and let his tongue loll in some wild and slightly disturbing doggy grin, possibly laying the foundations for a plea of "insanity". Everyone else just wondered "hang for what?"

The Chief Constable's aide whispered in one ear (one of the Chief Constable's ears, not one of Prince's).

'Since when?' the Chief Constable expostulated, legally and with due (scant) regard for PACE and what she usually described as "all of that namby-pamby bollocks".

The aide whispered some more and looked apologetic. The CC took a resigned-sounding deep breath.

'You bastards. You'll get *life* for this, all of you. With *hard labour*' she judged, in her best, deep, Sir Lancelot Spratt impression.

The Chief Constable's aide whispered in her ear again and then stepped smartly out of range, being averse to one-sided pugilism in the workplace. In *any* place, including face, groin and solar plexus.

'CHUFFING NANCY LILY-LIVERED WISHY-WASHY HUGGY-WUGGY BOLLOCKING LEFT-

WING LIBERAL BASTARD NONSENSE!' said the CC in an almost hypersonic squeak, her black-leather gloved hands flapping at her sides as though she were trying to rise into the air but had forgotten to wear her wings.

She continued her continually-revised speech, wholly unaware that she had in fact lost all gravitas, even in the eyes of Prince.

'You'll get *Psychoanalysis* and *Rehabilitation* for this, you *bastards*!'

The aide – suddenly looking happier – chanced yet another whisper into the Constabulary's Chief waxy, hairy ear-hole. The Chief Constable grinned.

'And the court of the press and the media will utterly *slay* you. We'll have your photographs and full identities and home addresses all over Twitface and Arsebook and VigilanteDotCom before you can look up how to spell a.n.o.n.y.m.i.t.y. Your lives as you knew them are over. O-ver. A plea of innocence is futile. We will add your biological and technological distinctiveness to our own. Your culture will adapt to service us.'

The Chief Constable then concentrated her gaze, unfocused, on some far horizon while she composed and transmitted a Press Release about how she'd cracked a sex gang slavery grooming ring gang slavery ring gang and how they were *all* male, pale and just as stale as expected according to Feminist Crime Theory so ner ner ne ner ner the Police *weren't* afraid to tackle gender and ethnic and gerontological minority crime and stick *that* up yer tabloids you cheap hacks. She rubbed her hands together and then indicated that the room ought to be cleared. 'Bzzzzzt!'

'BzzzzZZZZZZZZZZZZZzzzzzt!'

Bert was the first to be moved. At the top of the steps the Chief Constable leaned in and said 'When you get to the bottom you can explain to the Police Doctor how you tripped over your own feet.'

'Huh?' said Bert, before crashing down the staircase, bouncing off the walls and landing apex over fundament some distance from the bottom step. 'I'm alright – I'm fine. I must have tripped over my own feet or something' he said, wondering whether in the broken bone count "ribs" counted as one bone or as several. From where he lay he could see that Mr Dog – Prince - was the next one to trip over his own paws and descend a-la-canine-cartwheel, todging tackle over sniffing tackle and repeat until at a significantly lower altitude and also stationary.

Wheeeeee-thump-crash-roll-wuuuuuuffffffff-grrrrrrrrr-wowser-thump-crunch-roll-*splat*. Grrreat! Woof! Woof!

Prince, being a dog, thoroughly enjoyed the experience, and were it not for the handcuffs holding his front and back legs together, would have run back up the steps for another go. Instead he had to content himself with just panting and thinking to himself, once again, about the truly wonderful games that humans invented for him to play. This game was almost as good as that time he'd found a rope hanging from an old tree branch, a rope that he could hang onto with his teeth and swing out over the old sewage ponds. Then he went back to thinking more usual, less complicated thoughts. 'Dog. Dog. I'm a dog. Dog. Isn't everything great? Dog. Dog. I'm a dog. Ooh – great smell. Dog. When's dinner? Fart. Dog. Dog. Fart. Fart fart. Oops – got a doggy stiffy. Fart. OFFICER – I REALLY REALLY NEED TO LICK MY BALLS BUT I CAN'T REACH – I DON'T SUPPOSE THAT THERE'S ANY WAY THAT YOU WOULD CONSIDER... no, no, of course not. You also can't loosen the cuffs until we're back at the station. Dog. Dog dog dog dog dog dog dog DOGGGGGG. I need a shit. DOG! Food food food. Sniff.' That sort of thing.

Trial, as was customary in those parts of England (id est, all of it), was by Public Outrage and a Free Press composed of Virtue Signallers and Misandrists of All Eleventy-Ten

Mainstream Genders. It was no longer possible to be properly representative with a jury of a mere twelve.

Headline: 'Ten Men Involved In Proxy Canine Rape of Unconscious Woman's Leg Go Free Due To Scandalous Lack of Evidence. Only Dog Is Convicted. Chief Constable calls for a mis-trial and a summary execution in the Public Interest.'

A mob-rule.org petition has been raised by members of an Outraged Public demanding that the men be imprisoned anyway, so as not to continue to present a danger to any vulnerable women, or to their lickle bickle children, yeah, and this has already attracted ninety million signatures in England alone.

Parliament is working to introduce a bill to enact what has been dubbed "Sleeping Beauty's Law" to prevent further outrages such as the one (not) perpetrated by these men, and to protect *all* princesses from *any* form of abuse taking place between the kneecap and the ankle during slumber or casual naps.

A representative sample woman, who once had a man address her in rather off-hand and gruff tones, is reported to have said that she is "well chuffed" with the new *leg*-islation.

The dog involved is pictured here being driven off, with his head of out the window of the prison van, to begin his whole-of-life sentence at Belmarsh, or Dartmoor or somewhere where bastard evil criminals go. There it is believed that he will become the prison *bitch* and be buggered senseless on a frequent basis by the other prisoners and will come to know what it truly means to be a Feminist woman in a hostile and Patriarchal world.

Eight hundred Feminist Women have so far come forward to report that they too were subject to sexual assault by the dog, including two who were assaulted by the dog during the Crusades and one from the time of the last Ice Age.

The gang's ringleader, Bert "The Elbow Pervert" Smith, is said to have a long history of grabbing women's elbows as he pretends to be escorting his wife across busy roads.

Several other members of the gang are said to have been known to hold a woman's chair while she sits down, in order to ogle her buttocks. Police have not yet been able to trace the woman or the chair but enquiries will continue until they get to the bottom of the allegation.

Police have asked that any woman who was ever uncomfortable in the company of men or of dogs contact them immediately with lurid details and, if possible, grubby, creased, ill-lit Polaroid photographs of themselves looking care-free, physically-free and unspeakably happy in the company of their attacker.

The Princess remains in a stable condition and has been reported as "producing quite regular noises like a Gloucester Old Spot gagging on a bucketful of cold brawn", and "able to twitch her nostrils whenever an opened bottle of White Lightning is waved under her nose". her prognosis is said to be sweet dreams and fresh bedding each Monday and Thursday.

Anyone affected by any kind of discomfort at all at any point in their lives should seek professional medical and legal help.

Then they all lived happily ever after.

Jack and the Soy-BeanStalk

Near the Wearisome Woods on the outskirts of the relatively old new-town of Old Newtown there stood a ramshackle cottage. Ramshackle is perhaps the wrong word; it was a complete sodding dump, totally without charm or structural integrity. Generally you can verbally condemn such a property by referring to paintwork in need of attention, and to one or two missing tiles, a few weeds in the garden and an upside down Mk.I Ford Cortina Estate rusting into oblivion on the driveway. This cottage though was far, far beyond such criticism. The walls only remained upright because they'd all fallen towards one another at the same moment, and the roof would have been resting on the ground were it not for the fact that the walls had yet to finish collapsing. It was what an estate agent would describe as "an exciting investment opportunity".

The garden presented the local authorities with a bit of a dilemma. The cow seemed to indicate that the land might have status as a farm or small-holding, but there were ancient flower beds, relics from happier times, and these were so overgrown that two postmen had been lost, strangled by twists in the feral Russian Ivy creeping out from a trellis on the house wall. The Parish Council didn't know whether to send in the Army with grenades and flame-throwers or to award the place a generous cash grant and "site of special scientific interest" status.

There was damp rot, dry rot and Tommy rot. The drains, in similar fashion to the walls, had only refrained from collapsing because they were comprehensively blocked and the sewage pressure on the inside equalled the pressures from above and without.

Where once swallows had nested in the eaves and bats in the attic and rats in the cavity walls, the Rutland Society for the Protection of Birds, the Rutland Society for the Over-Indulgence of Bats, and the Rutland Society for the

Feather-Bedding of Rats had stepped in and re-homed them all on humanitarian grounds.

Jack Human lived in the cottage, with his mother. This is because there exists no such organisation as the Royal Society for the Mollycoddling of Jack, nor anything like it. Never has, like as not never will.

Jack's younger sister, Jill, had had it even worse than Jack.

Jill had long since been forced to refrain from toting pails of water up and down the hill, by the Royal Society for Women & You-Go-Girls. Jill had been tricked (with the award of higher marks from teachers and examiners, and from some pretty rotten blanket encouragement, it must be said) into doing and being anything that her little heart desired (so long as it wasn't toting pails of water up and down hills – that was verboten). University (B.A. Gender Studies, M.A. Equality for Women, and PhD. Non-Binary Women as a Sub-Culture in Patriarchal Romantic Literature) scarred Jill for life, and she found herself conscripted into a well-paid, sedentary professional position in The City where, although she didn't have time for a man or children in her life, she *did* have plenty of money with which to buy luxury food and toys for her (indoor only) cats.

Jack's mother got blankets too. Blanket plaudits and credit – mostly Child Credit - and Methadone prescriptions for doing the best that any woman possibly could under the circumstances, these circumstances being fifty percent responsibility for getting knocked up and zero responsibility accepted for the child that the *In Camera* Family Court insisted *must* stay with his mother, because *mother*, yeah? Aw bless! Like Ms God, the Patriarchy works in mysterious ways.

Jack was by then in his mid-twenties as the year flies, but he had an emotional and intellectual age of "tricycle", not through any clinical pathology, but because he'd never been allowed to play with children of his own species, never had an adult that he could look up to in anyway except by physically by bending his neck upwards to receive a tongue lashing. In The Age of Stupid it was, in fact, not a foregone conclusion that there actually *were* any children of Jack's species. Jack, like everyone else except old white men (and young white men, and middle-aged white men too, who were *all* just horrible), was unique.

Jack was in effect a species of one while at home.

Jack's mother was, in effect, a *right one*, as everyone in the neighbourhood knew but none might say for fear of the Unthink Notspeak Police arriving. Jack's mother had many interests and many social connections, few of them her own.

Jack's life hitherto before and preceding our little tale herein told had consisted largely of locking himself in his room, listening to the most awful music imaginable on headphones and trying to wank himself to death. He was well on the road to success; his eyesight was on the myopic side of *mole* and the palms of his hands were hairier than a brown bear's bum in wintertime. He was still working on the *death* bit of his plan.

Jack stood in front of the mirror in his room, looked himself up and down and showed his approval of himself with a quick round of jazz-hands. He wore low-cut skinny (red) jeans (short enough to show pasty, thin, ankle), canvas deck shoes (blue), a pre-ripped t-shirt bearing the slogan 'This is what a Feminist looks like [these days]'. He sported a very wispy beard (the blessed oestrogen was strong in this one), studious, heavy-framed spectacles - and hair just perfect (an asymmetrical cut obscuring one eye). Had Jack been on the stage – please don't put *your* daughter on the stage, Mrs Worthington – his name on the billing would have been Anne-Dee Drogyny; Fashion-Victim Incarnate.

'Feck – I'm *gorgeous!*' he muttered to himself and turned to look over his shoulder at the rear of his ensemble. Baggy-arse folds of denim where his sitting-down-comfortably-without-a-cushion equipment ought to have been, weak shoulders, torso so skinny that you could see the bulges of his kidneys, legs like a stork that's just shat itself. 'Perfect!' he concluded. Hardly any hint of toxic mannishness present at all.

Jack pouted and wondered seriously about lipstick, but he wasn't yet brave enough or confident within his public body-self-declarations for that. The goth-black statement-stick would have to stay where it was hidden at the back of his sock drawer for a while yet. Talking of which... he checked that no-one was about to walk in on him and pushed a rolled-up pair down the front of his jeans. Then he took them out again – he'd be mortified if they slipped out accidentally, and besides – he didn't want to rely on anything false. Jack was nothing if not totally himself at all times, he told himself, in the lazy soprano that he'd learned to affect, with an upward inflection on every sentence akin to a question mark that ought properly to not be there?

Hackney's bedroom was directly opposite Jack's, separated by a hallway stacked floor to ceiling with old newspapers and black plastic sacks of used cat-litter that she couldn't bear to part with.

Hackney was Jack's mother.

Hackney's parents had been hoping for a shag in Chelsea or Kensington, but neither of them had had the necessary bus fare, so they'd shagged in Hackney and gone their different ways.

It had all been quite beautiful really, except that the Law of The Land at the time specified that if there was a ickle bay-bay after you'd shagged you had to name it after *where* you'd shagged. Misunderstanding this a lot of kids grew up called 'Bathroom' and 'Back Seat ov a Mini' and 'Toilet Cubicle', but Hackney's parent was brighter than this, and they had shagged right next to a sign that had read 'Hackney Borough Council – Bill Posters will be prosecuted'.

No, Hackney didn't have any middle names (although she *did* have a distant half-brother called Bill Posters).

Jack's grandmother, Tower-Hamlets Nick, had stood near the vandalised bus shelter in the pouring rain, crying out with not some little passion as her beau, Dagenham Dog-Races, had been driven away by the Metropolitan Rozzers in the Paddy Wa... in the Black Mar... um, in the *Police Van*.

'Let 'im go you bloody rotten bar-stards, 'e was wiv me when that ol' lady got whacked an' she didn't 'ave no money in 'er bag anyways so it wont even wurf it. I'M PREGGERS!'

A craggy and wild heath or remote and windy moorland just couldn't have played host to the depth of emotions involved in quite the way that the bombed-out Woolworths behind the vandalised bus shelter did. Ms Tower-Hamlets never saw Mr Dagenham again but, when she was fifteen, little Hackney had been born. Hackney followed in mummy's stiletto-steps, and just another fifteen years after that, out had popped Jack.

Jack had been a little surprise really. Hackney, not being au fait with her own pelvic geography, had pushed and strained, expecting a huge and intransigent turd, not a little bay-bay. Blow me, she thought as she looked down, she didn't know that her front-bottom could even *do* that. So *that* was where bay-bays came from! E-ew! Hackney had flushed and flushed and flushed, but little Jack was a survivor, he just wouldn't disappear down the lav, slowly climbing up the umbilical cord like a rat up a Port Said mooring rope.

Decades of loving domesticity and child-care later, at just the one and the same moment that Jack stepped from his bedroom, a gentleman who looked as though he had been caught in an explosion at an ironmongers and whose ambulance had then crashed at speed into a tattoo parlour was coming out of Jack's beloved mummy's room.

They both stopped, slightly embarrassed to have encountered one another.

'Mgghh' said Jack.

'Mgghh-unhh' replied the other, not waiting for the Google translation of Jack's presumed greeting to come through.

The stranger, not knowing the routine of the house, felt that more was necessary when it really was not. 'My name's Tony. I, er, I know your mother... um...'

'...Hackney' said Jack, helpfully filling in the gap in Tony's declared knowledge of his mother.

Another man appeared behind Tony, zipping up his jeans.

'Mgghh'ing' said the other man, looking at Tony and then at Jack.

Tony completed the introductions. 'This is Dave. Your mother's a very popular woman.'

There fell then a kind of uneasy quiet upon the little group, as Dave hopped up and down, persuading his boots onto his bare feet.

Tony broke the moment. 'Off to school?' he asked Jack, aware that if there were children in the house that that was just the sort of question they liked to be asked by men they'd never seen before who were coming out of their mother's bedroom in a state of sartorial disarray and sexual satiety.

'No' replied Jack. 'Market. I'm off to market.'

'Lovely' said Dave. 'I love Margate. Good class of bird in Margate. Shag guaranteed.'

Tony slapped him around the back of the pony-tail, and they all shuffled past one another, to be on their various ways before *fings* got even more uncomfortable.

Jack popped his head through his mother's bedroom door, thinking to tell her that he was taking the cow to Margate – um, taking the cow to *market*. One more head-sized hole in the door wouldn't matter, and for Jack the plywood-and-deal-frame based violence with its promise of self-harm was cathartic.

Mummy told Jack to piss off because Mummy was busy. She was indeed busy, veins not being easy to come by at this late stage of her career, especially with a needle that had been blunted by serving the needs of the community-at-large for some several months. If only Mummy had retained the ability to perambulate independently after the sexual attentions of Dave and Tony she might have nipped around to the alleyway at the back of the Post Office to scout around on the tarmac for a fresher needle, but no, Jack's mummy didn't think she'd be able to walk again until at least Coronation Street or Eastenders, and at that perhaps not even that day's episodes.

Jack, backing out of the doorway, was then disturbed, not so much by his mother looking like something that a giant cat had coughed up on a damp mattress dumped under a motorway fly-over, but by the sound of a Subaru Impreza Turbo with huge boost-dump valve and 2,000 watt stereo with subwoofers cranking over in the garden and starting up – with a background melody of cow moo.

Daisy!

Jack got outside in time to see Tony and Dave manhandling Daisy upside down into the boot of the Subaru, her hooves poking out and her udders dangling over the number plate like a poorly-inflated sex toy for lonely dairy farmers.

'Oi! That's our cow!'

Tony, tying the boot lid down with a bungee cord, explained that, no, Daisy was no longer their cow. 'Your mother bought a bit o'gear last night. If there's any change

105

due when we get Daisy paid into abattoir we'll send you a pint.'

Dave asked Tony how many packets of streaky bacon were in the average cow, and Tony pushed Dave into the car and slammed the passenger door by way of answer. Surely everyone knew that bacon came from sheep?

The Subaru, all four wheels spinning wildly, then left for pastures urban and it left only just in time; the Russian Ivy had already secured quite a firm grip on the rear spoiler and its false number-plate. The rear suspension already had its work cut out for it, not being set up for "cow". The home-made exhaust system scraped along the roadway, leaving a trail of quite the brightest sparks, all things considered, for many miles around.

Jack stood in the garden and just didn't know what to do. Daisy had been their only source of income since the benefit fraud debacle – and they hadn't exactly been creaming it in. However would they survive now that Daisy had gone, her cash value making its way across the ocean towards Colombia in a perfect example of trickle-up global drugs industry economics?

Suddenly Jack smiled. 'I know' he said to himself. 'I'll open an account at the Food Bank and take out a loan.'

Jack, through some quite clever rhythmic use of his legs and feet, made his way to the nearest Food Bank and joined the queue. This wasn't really such a clever feat of navigation as might first seem, since the Food Bank was the only institution still in business on the High Street. It wasn't even that far to the back of the queue really, just a long way from there to the Food Bank itself. Jack was in a frazzle by the time he had shuffled forward sufficiently for the building to be within sight, and he'd had to Tweet "hashtag-traumatised" several times. By the time he reached the doorway of the Food Bank he'd been reduced to sharing weepy selfies of himself after being repeatedly beaten up by the nice ladies in the queue. When the female of the species puts the boot in they really put it in, and one or two of them had to be helped to get it out again.

The woman at the desk didn't actually ask Jack why he was upset and crying, but he just knew that she wanted to know, so he told her anyway.

'The queue – they're all so, like – hostile, yeah? Why are they so hostile?'

The woman looked up and her expression suggested that she'd been continuously pissing acid and shitting barbed wire since staggering out of the Rift Valley and evolving into a charity worker.

'We get a lot of men – single men – thinking that they need to eat too. It diverts charity resources from the truly needy. Referral?'

'What?'

'Your letter of referral, signed by two General Practitioners, your Social Work caseworker and at least one Bishop not yet accused or convicted of paedophilia, bestiality or putting sticky fingers in the collection plate. Come on, we haven't got all day.'

'I don't know any bishops. Our cow was stolen this morning. Daisy.'

'Don't call me Daisy. Cow? Stolen?'

'Well, two men that did big sex naughties on my mummy all night last night took our cow in payment for mummy's drug debts. They put her in the boot of their Subaru and sped off.'

'They put your mother in the boot of a Subaru?'

'No, the cow. Mummy's at home, fried out of her brains and wondering why her lady-bits are itching again.'

The lady looked as though she'd passed just a little bit more acid-for-pee, and was gophering some barbed wire. 'Three forms of ID' she said.

Thinking that this was some sort of general knowledge question to test his IQ Jack replied 'Um – Driving Licence, Passport and a Letter from the Police stating that no further action will be taken at this time due to lack of living witnesses.' He looked pleased with himself and wondered what he'd won.

'Piss off.'

'Beg pardon?'

'Piss off' said the nice charity woman again. 'You live on a farm, you've got money for drugs, you're wearing a pair of designer pre-ripped jeans that must have cost a hundred and fifty quid, and all morning my phone has been beeping with you whining on Twitter about having to queue to get in here – with each tweet marked as "Sent from my iPhone model MCMLXXVII". If you're going hungry then I'm a Dutchman.'

Jack wasn't sure how to react, being anxious to impart the truth as best he could in what was rapidly becoming difficult circumstances again.

'Boop de floop di boogie oogie woogie flerp de doop?' he ventured. 'A *v*indmill in olde Amshterdam? My other car is a DAF 33? Oops I *dink* I have *clogged* the *toy*-let?' he said.

'Get lost, I'm busy' said the lady on reception. 'There are genuinely needy people waiting'. The front end of the queue gave her a resounding round of "jazz hands" in approval. A cynic would have noticed that the queue appeared to have been selected with just one, United Nations approved, gender in mind. Jack, had he but known the ropes, would have done better to self-identify as *Ze/Zie*.

Or even as Zsa Zsa Gabor.

Jack hesitated at the door, unused to such rejection and still trying his best to understand. 'Pass the dutchie on the lef' hand side?' he said, hoping to establish some sort of rapport that might yield at minimum a tin of beans.

A small tin of something tasty and nutritious from Messrs Heinz (U.K.) Limited hit him on the head.

'Thank you he cried' as he cried, overcome not so much with emotion as with a pressing need for at least three stitches in his scalp. So, he thought, Food Banks *do* work for single men, but it *was* a largely unfathomable process and very slow, and he wasn't at all sure that his skull was up to the work involved in being awarded a full week's worth of man-groceries.

An old woman who looked as though she'd lived her entire life in a shoe or something tugged at his sleeve as he staggered away. 'Next time, love, borrow some kids - and dress more convincingly as a woman' she advised, giving him the confidential nod. 'You're almost there, you just need to find a pair of falsies and use a bit o' lipstick.'

Jack, not knowing what else to do, took a "selfie" with her and her seventeen, rather disparate-looking children. The children were all tied together with a rather long shoe-lace.

Jack took the (dented) tin of *Baked GM Num-Num Beans in Tomato-Flavoured Red Sauce* home, and he left them on the kitchen table so that when she regained consciousness, Mummy would know that he'd not wasted his day. He must then have fallen asleep with exhaustion or something, the author doesn't know the details, but it was some hours later when he wandered back through to the kitchen. Mummy was there, her head slumped on the yellow Formica of the table next to an empty can of Heinz Baked Beanz. No dinner for Jack then, he deduced. Aw bless! His very first independent deduction, oh how quickly he was growing up!

Mummy woke up.

Mummy looked at Jack through glazed and sleepy eyes, and she smiled.

Mummy rushed to the kitchen window and vomited part-digested baked beans into the garden.

Mummy then went to sleep again, still hanging part way in and part way out of the window.

Mummy had forgotten to put quite all of her clothes on, so Jack, very gingerly, covered up some of mummy with an old tea-towel. Then he went back to his room and, after a brief but satisfying three-sock wank while thinking about the lady at the food bank reception feeding him Pot Noodles while they did big sex on each other, he cried himself to sleep. Jack was quite fond of fantasies of some domination, and it turned him on to think of it making up for the past abuses of all of the horrid bad, testosterone-laden toxic man-mens. Plus, it was much more comfortable just lying on his back and letting someone else do all of the work, even when it was just imagined sex.

Next morning as he awoke time became confused for Jack and he wasn't sure for a moment whether the sound of a Subaru Impreza had featured in the tail-end of his dreams or whether it had really awoken him. A note on the kitchen table clarified matters. Mummy had gone.

'Drivin to Ibeefa wiv Dayve an Tonny fora oliday. Dont frow my stuff away you barstard. As Sooperman sayed in that film u like I'll be back. Luv U Mumsy.'

'Pee-ess, dont wank yourself to deaf or youll go blind an we r not avin a giyde dog.'

'Pee-pee-ess, also do somefink about the garden you lazy twat. Itz overgrowed overnight.'

The kitchen *did* seem to be remarkably less well-lit than was usual. Jack wasn't certain but he wondered whether the lack of daylight entering might have something to do with the enormous soy-beanstalk that had appeared and matured overnight, right where Mummy had vomited beans yesterday. He went outside for a better look.

The beanstalk was wide, wider than Jack could spread his arms, and it disappeared all the way up into the clouds. Huge leaves on strong stalks sprang from its sides, almost as though Father Nature had designed the beanstalk with an external spiral staircase!

'Well I never!' expostulated Jack, scratching the bones where his arse ought rightly to be.

'Later perhaps, kid' said the Council Planning Officer who had crept up behind Jack, summoned there by the telephone calls of Jack's neighbours who feared that the beanstalk would deleteriously affect local property prices, reducing them from two farthings to just one. 'For the moment though you can show me your PCF-211/179d Triplicated beige flimsy.'

'Huh?' said Jack, intelligently.

'Planning consent form. For this whatever it is.'

'Planning consent?' said Jack, slightly less intelligently still.

'His type never have it' offered the Council Infestation Engineer who had crept up on them both, summoned by the neighbours who were worried because aphids, scaled to match the width and height of the beanstalk, were occasionally falling from it and sucking the partly-digested intestines out of pet cats and goats and things.

'I don't have it' said Jack, back on his intellectual terra firma. Jack was used to explaining about things that he didn't have. There wasn't much that Jack did have, really. Not until that morning, anyway, when suddenly he found himself in loco without a parent present, and in possession of an excessively enthusiastic growth from which aphids were falling and some sort of sap leaking. A ladybird the size of Daisy the cow scuttled down to ground level to feed on a particularly good dribble of sticky sap. Then it scuttled back up into the clouds.

'Coccinellidae Bugger-Me That's Enormous, to give it its full Latin name, if I'm not mistaken' announced a gentleman from the R.S.P.C.A. who had been summoned by the neighbours, who had begun to lose old and infirm *human* members of their extended families to the aphids, and who didn't like the mess that was left over. 'Ladybirds in England, although our 'Merrycan cousins call them "Lady*bugs*", I believe. Devastating enough when just the more usual few millimetres but I suspect that when cow-sized as here they could devastate whole forests. Something will have to be done.'

A ladybird approached the little group from the roadway, excused itself, and crept back up the beanstalk, carrying a large but – to be honest – rather imperfectly formed golden Labrador dog in its chitinous mouth-parts, trailing a sight-challenged and somewhat annoyed gentleman waving a white stick around as though it were some sort of cutlass.

'Full payment within seven days' said a representative of the Guide Dogs for the Blind Association, who had been alerted by the neighbours to an old gentleman and his dog being attacked by an enormous insect. 'These dogs aren't cheap to train, you know.' He passed a rather large bill to Jack and filed the carbon copy to the back of the pad clipped to his clipboard clip. Replacing his peaked cap on his head he then went off to investigate reports of abuse of a Fetching Monkey for the Lazy in the Dolce Vita high-rise towers on the other side of town.

A rather concerned neighbour appeared and stood rather close to the beanstalk, looking up. 'Police ought to do something. Someone could be killed by something falling out of this thing.'

Just then an elderly gentleman, still waving a white stick around as though it were a pirate cutlass, fell out of the beanstalk and onto the neighbour, saving himself from further physical injury but extinguishing the life of the concerned neighbour in a most emphatic manner. Such is the tragedy of receiving almost immediate empirical proof, sometimes, which is just one reason why we ought all to be careful what we say and to whom and when and, in particular, where.

'I must ask you to take immediate action, my lad, immediate action to prevent further loss of life' said the Policeman in rather gruff tones, reaching into a pocket for his Death by Amusing Causes pad, arranging the carbon-paper for two copies, and licking the end of his HB pencil stub.

'Nick him!' shouted a ne'er-do-well from the sidelines, hoping to incite a riot (there being nothing good on the telly).

'Hang him!' called the ne'er-do-well's mother, joining in the spirit of things.

'Burn him!' shouted someone carrying a flaming brand. Odd, isn't it, how we always stick to our lasts?

A fireman, who had crept up on them all by dint of not using the engine's awoogah-awoogah wah-wah hee-honk hee-honk aural warning device, added his two pennyworth to the reasoned debate. 'Never play with matches, children, and remember that Smokey The Bear *does* do big shits in the woods. Once you've burned him your local Fire Brigade is ready and waiting to cool down the embers and prevent accidental spread of any subsequent bright sparkery.'

Jack found himself backing towards the beanstalk. 'You're all being really rather rotten' he cried. 'Mummy swapped our cow for drugs and now she's gone away with two men she's been having something called "a spit-roast threesome" with and the Food Bank only gave me one small tin of beans and Mummy ate those and I'm all alone and I think I've wet myself and nobody cares.'

'That's about right' said one of Jack's more reasonable neighbours. 'We don't give a shit. Kick the little snowflake's teeth in! Wait until the pee on his jeans dries – and then burn him! Better fire that way, can't burn damp snowflakes. Too much smoke.'

'Aye' agreed a studious young lady who had ridden up quietly on a vast Triumph motorcycle with green strobe lights, catching them all by surprise until she took her helmet off and shook her golden locks free and back into shape. She was from the Social Work Department's Emergency Response Team. 'Little bastards like him are just a drain on resources. He's been conning things out of the local Food Bank. Burn him! Kick his teeth in and then burn him *and* his teeth. Damn the smoke – this is an emergency! Burn him while he's still damp!'

Jack rubbed his eyes and choked back a sob, stretching out his favourite t-shirt at the nipples, so that the young lady could read the legend. 'But – I'm a feminist. I'm one of you... I *am* what a feminist looks like...'

There was the sound of a match being struck, and I don't mean an emotional match between the author and Chris Pratt, damn it, I mean one of the phosphorus kind.

'I'm sorry! I'm so sorry!' cried Jack. 'I'll do better in future! I'm sorry I'm sorry I'm sorry!'

'Sorry? What for?' asked the elderly, vision-challenged gentleman who had fallen out of the beanstalk and who had landed quite fortuitously on the concerned but now deceased neighbour, and who was still wondering how his dog had suddenly got them both fifty feet up in the air and then let go – and who still, for obvious reasons, hadn't a clue what was going on but was still waving his white stick around like a pirate cutlass anyway, just in case.

'I'm sorry for *everything*!' sobbed Jack. 'For this beanstalk and for the British Empire and for my Toksvig masculinity and for being non-ethnic and for not being a woman and for living off the proceeds of slavery and for being the violent half of the species and for my systemic privilege and...'

'SYSTEMIC?' screamed a(nother) neighbour, now also as concerned as the recently deceased concerned neighbour in a mangled heap under the soy-beanstalk. 'Aaaaargggghh!'

'What does "systemic" mean then?' enquired someone who wasn't from the neighbourhood at all but who had just been passing by in the hopes of nicking something half decent which only goes to prove that ambition is relative.

'It's a medical word, innit. It means his *whole system's* diseased.'

'KILL HIM! KILL HIM WITH FIRE WHILE WE STILL CAN!' shouted the Fireman, whose professional year to date had, in truth, been two logs short of a decent conflagration, and who wasn't convinced that he could remember how to make the big foam nozzle on the hand-cart work but wanted an excuse to try.

Jack turned and scrambled up the beanstalk, stepping from leaf to leaf, the poorly-cut gusset of his baggy-arsed skinny-leg jeans threatening to destroy his trembling little testicles as he did so. Two more ladybirds and a confused carrot-worm fell past him as he climbed.

Soon Jack's head was in the clouds. I mean for real this time, not just that he was generally dippy. He was really up there in the fluffy stuff. It was about as far away from the rabbit hole that he'd ever been in his entire life. Why oh why, he whined, did escaping from pseudo-Marxist identity-politics driven wholly proscriptive misandrist feminist-ideologue gynocentric gangs issuing threats of immolation always involve climbing swiftly from one branch of some tree to a higher branch, pause and repeat, until stopped by lack of oxygen and/or a red-pill epiphany?

Far below, gathered around the trunk of the soy-beanstalk, the mob was incensed that another inherently-privileged white boy had escaped justice by the cunning use of a relatively high-velocity non-sanctioned arboreal hate *movement*, to wit a departure modelled on cultural appropriation of the historical tree-climbing activities of unreconstructed young ethnic non-females indigenous to forested environments. It's in the genes, they all agreed, even though most of Jack's (admittedly skinny and bony) arse was patently *not* in his jeans as he climbed. You could have parked a small unicycle in there, so long as you weren't going to need to sniff the wheel afterwards for quite some time.

News got out fast that a privileged young white man was on the *official* run, and it took Jack half an hour and more to climb above the flight-ceiling of the aeroplanes scrambled by the R.A.F. to try to shoot him down. Jack stopped once in a while for a breather, and to shake a little fist at his pursuers. Oh how Jack wished that he was somewhere else, such as hanging onto the Empire State Building perhaps, while shaking his little fist at bi-planes buzzing around him. Anywhere but in this dystopian organic nightmare of Nature perverted beyond recognition.

Fortunately, as everyone on Earth knows, Heinz Beanz are just pure magic. What on earth would earth would like if a million housepersons every day picked up a tin of beans and, say, vomited them out of their kitchen windows just as Mummy had done? Jack was careful not to think about bears because as they do say, it just doesn't bear thinking about. Magic cannot be explained, only experienced. A million sons of single mothers a day climb up a soy-beanstalk grown from one small tin and say 'Bugger me, it's a long way down. I want my daddy.'

Some opinionated old twat who liked to present himself as a really groovy hippy went past in his space-balloon and threw rocks, yelling something about "lack of diversity in beanstalk climbers" and "my staff are my greatest asset, that's why you're all on unpaid leave starting now" and "give billionaire bail-outs a chance". The silly old twat then looped the loop, lost his grip on his dentures and had to dive dive dive to chase after them. Jack was free and alone and safe from the world, far, far above it all, beyond the many traps of the trappings of modern civilisation.

Jack's head, still bruised and tender from the award of a tin of Baked Beans, then thumped rather hard and *very* unexpectedly into a wooden trap-door. No idea what happened to the soy-beanstalk, you'll just have to accept that this sort of thing happens in old folk tales. Think of it as you might think of the ever-present inescapable non-sequitur of Feminist "Logic" in "debates".

Poppy doopy doopy doopy do climb climb climb - THUD – total and inexplicable change of scenery. Soy-beanstalk one moment, underside of a whole world in the sky the next.

'Hashtag WTF?' said Jack, not knowing why but thinking that it sounded rather good. If only there had been someone there to hear his witty outburst. 'Colour me surprised' he said, then thoroughly on a quip-roll.

His legs were tired and his clothes were stained with beanstalk juice and his hands, well – he didn't want to dwell on it but his hands were crusted with ladybird poo. In his defence he hadn't been fondling ladybird bottoms or anything, it was just that they left poo everywhere and it was impossible to climb the soy-beanstalk without getting covered in red and black polka-dot shite.

I tell you, if that trap-door had been just a tiny bit harder to push open than it was then Jack wouldn't have made it through. He'd probably just have sat there on a leaf at the top of the beanstalk, sobbing, until he'd fallen off. As things were though the trap-door was well-designed, well-constructed, well-balanced and the hinges lightly oiled as part of a continuous preventative-maintenance routine. Maintenance of the infrastructure of the land in the sky had *not* been contracted out to the lowest possible bid, but was still tended to by a man in overalls with an oil can, a rag and secure employment in an honourable and respected trade.

Jack climbed up and through the trap-door and found himself in The Land in the Sky, a land where blue-sky thinking was the norm and where absolutely nobody did any thinking at all if they were inside a box. The trap-door had opened up in the middle of a green pasture where the grass was greener, much, much greener, than the green,

green grass of home (especially now that Daisy was no longer around to spread fertiliser all over it).

Because he *wasn't* in a box Jack was free to think both 'WTF?' *and* 'TBH – it all looks a bit *big*' to himself. Even though they were his own thoughts, Jack didn't really understand them when he heard them, and he frightened himself a little bit in his jeans. It is for experiences just such as this that men designed domestic washing machines to have that one odd two-and-a-half-hour cycle that doesn't stint on water-usage or electricity to heat it.

Jack was just admiring the smaller-*looking* distant scenery and the smaller-*looking* distant mountains and castles when two very *big*-looking giants strode up, taking seven-league strides. One of them peered down at him and then picked him up by his left foot.

'Funny little bloke here, Bert' said Sidney, holding his own head downside up as best he could for a better view, as both giants and dogs are wont to do when puzzled by something.

'Christ, what's he dressed as?'

'Now Bert, don't make fun, he be one o' they metropolitan types, all funky and hip.'

'Soy-boy? Hipster?'

'Waister (sic), more like, he's 'orribly underfed.'

'Make someone a good *waif* then one day you reckon?'

'Ba-dum tish. No, Bert – *this* be a young male feminist.'

'Oh – a streak o'piss. Gotcha. A fool, a *cretin* in fact, a useful unwitting dumb tool in the misandrist activities of the political hate-movement that is *Feminism*.'

'Thazzit.'

They turned Jack around and around to get a better look, and they only sniggered just a little at Jack's outfit, and only then when he was turned to face away. Jack, aware that he was twenty feet off the "ground", held between finger and thumb of some enormous beast, and vaguely conscious that he looked a little bit wussy in comparative juxtaposition to their work-a-day outfits, crossed his arms over the 'This Is What A Feminist Looks Like' legend on his t-shirt. His arms were a bit skinny but they covered most of the lettering.

Eventually Sidney spoke to Jack. 'Don't worry lad, first things first let's get you properly dressed like a *bloke* and then I'll bet you're a bit hungry after your climb, aren't you?'

Jack admitted that he was, and Sidney put him in the front pocket of his checked shirt. Bert closed the trap-door (after clearing his throat and gobbing a reasoned socio-political and philosophical argument down through it first). Far below the assembled righteous throng agreed amongst themselves that it felt like heavy rain or sleet or something was on the way, but still none of them were quite sufficiently prepared, physically or mentally, for when it arrived. This was especially so because the rain when it arrived, arrived as one big lump, and there were pipe-tobacco yellow streaks and fruit-of-the-nose green bits in the middle of it.

Bert whispered a giant whisper to Sidney. 'Mark my words, he'll be after a tofu salad and a skinny coconut-milk latté with lemon.'

Sidney shushed him again and addressed Jack.

'Steak and chips, pint of beer?'

Jack had no idea what those things were, but they sounded splendid. It was the first time that a grown man – even a giant man – had spoken to Jack conversationally, and he responded like a domestic dog; more to the tone of voice than to the words.

Bert couldn't resist. 'Avocado on raisin-bran toast and a small glass of alcohol-free Chablis?'

Jack had no idea what those things were either, but they too sounded splendid. Jack had never been at the *expense-account* end of the Useful Dumb Tool Male Feminist career path.

In no time at all (because of the giants' seven-league strides) the three of them were in the Great Dining Hall of the best, most solid-looking castle in the whole giant valley. Jack found himself sitting on the table, on the edge of a vast serving platter while Sidney hovered over him with a carving knife and meat-fork, looking for the tastiest bits.

The beef joint under Sidney's scrutiny towered high over Jack's head, and Jack's feet were carelessly dipped into the warm onion gravy at its base. Sidney, having decided that it was *all* good, danced around with the carving knife, trying to elicit a clue from Jack as to whether he wanted a big bit of meat or a *stupidly* big bit of meat. When he finally sliced into the joint and cut off a thick slice the size of a court-confiscated and crushed Subaru it fell with a plop into the meaty-juices gravy goodness and soaked Jack from head to foot.

A buxom serving wench of the castle who had in no way been forced into a B.S.W. career but who in fact liked the hours, the lack of paperwork and lack of corporate responsibility, put her tray of beers down. Heck, she even liked the uniform! She laughed (there was never any question of her being prevented from doing so at any time) and she grabbed Jack and licked the gravy off him, sucking his feet to get the little lumpy bits from between his toes. Jack promptly came in his pants and thus could no longer be considered a total virgin. The serving wench (Daphne) dunked Jack into a vast mug of frothy beer, gave him a quick shake to dry him off and set him down on his own plate, among the petits pois, his back resting on a very warm crusty roast potato and with an elbow propped up on a Yorkshire pudding. She'd obviously played with dolls (or younger brothers – same thing really) as a child.

This was turning out to be Jack's best day ever, but he was still tongue tied. He grinned and he squirmed, only able to glance up a couple of very furtive times.

Bert asked Daphne 'Got any clothes to fit him? Something better than these soy-boy fop-swabs? He looks as though he was dressed by someone who couldn't get into Art College.'

Daphne reckoned she could run something up, given his measurements and an uninterrupted half an hour with the old pedal-powered Singer.

'Tiny pair of Levi 501s, denim shirt, black Donkey Jacket do him? He'll have to go commando, and you can use the boots off one of your Action Man dolls, Sidney. I've lost the pattern for half-inch boxer shorts, and unless you're talking horseback-with-whip and the lads from the stables I don't do leatherwork.'

'Perfick' said Bert, and gave Daphne a pinch on the bum. Bert and Daphne had been co-habiting under the blessings of Vicar, Town Clerk and both sets of parents since before – well, since long before the castle got indoor plumbing. A while.

Sidney blushed a little at the mention of his collection of Action Man figures. Seriously, they were from his childhood, he'd just never got around to throwing them away or putting them up for sale on the internet.

Jack was busying himself on his plate, having a huge pea before falling backwards, very theatrically, into his mashed potato. He'd not eaten like this since – no, he'd *never* eaten like this, with more than one thing on his plate at the same time. Heck, he'd rarely eaten off plates at all. Mummy's best Sunday lunch offering was, occasionally, a packet of crisps and a box of SunnyD with a bent straw.

Presently – a common fairy/folk-tale term meaning "later" – when Jack's meal had barely been touched and Jack was lying semi-comatose, his head resting on an upturned Yorkshire pudding while his stomach fumbled for fresh gut-gussets and antacids, Daphne returned with his new clothing. Sidney woke Jack by poking him ever so gently with a bone-marrow scoop, and bade him dress. Jack took a little privacy by finding himself behind a half-full claret jug. When he reappeared he sported the biggest grin on his face since – well, since *ever*.

'Thank you, Daphne' he said, in a very shy little voice.

Daphne winked at him, looked him up and down and then growled like a *ti*ger. Jack's vision narrowed, darkness crept in at the edges and there was the most awful high-pitched note in his head. He fought with himself, determined not to faint. Daphne was going to feature in a lot of Jack's daydreams for quite some time to come.

True to her word Daphne had kitted Jack out with properly-fitting blue jeans, a darker blue denim shirt that would withstand a nuclear blast, and a black donkey-jacket of the sort that dustmen used to wear when men doing essential manual labour was still something celebrated and respected, not belittled and derided. With the boots appropriated from one of Sidney's Action Men figures Jack immediately walked a few inches taller. Stepping out beyond the cruet set Jack met with approval from Sidney *and* from Bert.

'Proper little gentleman.'

'Feels better already, eh? Not like such a prissy little wuss?'

Jack nodded.

'Pub, I think' said Sidney. 'Time we introduced you to the rest of the lads.'

Jack was running in the red. Blokes – blokes who wanted to include him socially!

The pub, next to the castle, was just your average timber-framed, white-painted, thatched-roof , thousand-year-old English inn affair serving a vast selection of independently-brewed beers and ales. An old, painted wooden sign swung over the door and Jack wondered if the establishment was under Chinese ownership – The Fe Fi Fo Fum Arms seemed to be such an unlikely name otherwise.

The motif appeared to be a large and sniffy-looking nose over crossed plasma-bag and intravenous drip stands.

Inside though, oh, inside – a roaring fire in the hearth, perfect lighting (wall-lamps, just a little bit yellowed from centuries of inventive-ingredient pipe-tobacco smoke) and the atmosphere a healthy spectrum from pure and clean at floor-level to full nicotine-fog at (giant) head-height.

The conversational buzz died the moment that Sidney entered with Jack sitting on his shoulder, and silence fell. The pub's dogs got to their feet and they stood, tails held still and high, standing and staring like standing dogs staring with their tails held still and high, trying to decide whether Jack was some new squeaky-toy for them to play with or a giant in the puppy stage.

Then a great roar went up as Jack was welcomed. Giant after giant made as though to slap Jack on the back but then thought better of it, not wanting to smear him across Sidney's shoulder. Barker and Dobson, the pub's dogs, stood then on their hind legs for a better sniff, their tails stirring the warm fog. A path was cleared for the party so that they could get to the bar.

'Got any I.D.?' said the landlord.

Bert fumbled in a vast pocket for his Giant O.A.P. Bus Pass. Bert's Bus Pass had originally been issued as a New-Fangled Horse & Cart Pass. Bert was well old. Methusaloid.

'No, I meant him – has he got any I.D.?'

Jack had remembered to transfer his meagre possessions over from his old clothes to his new, and he produced his (old, expired) Probation Services Cafe Discount Card. The landlord plugged a jeweller's loupe into his eye socket and peered.

'Well, Jack, Son of Dagenham, over the age of consent and thus welcome in my licensed premises, what'll you have?'

The pub fell once more to silence. One of the pub dogs, both self-determining and independent sorts, the who had been darning a dog's hind-leg sock, dropped a pin. Once the clanging of the pin died away only the crackle of the logs burning in the grate remained.

A voice thundered out from one of the alcoves. 'Dagenham? *Son* of *Dagenham*?'

Jack bit his lip and trembled. 'S'my name, yes. Daddy went away before I was borned, but that was his name. Mummy was left all by herself to brung me up all by herself up yes.'

The giant who had spoken approached. 'I am Dagenham. Was your mother's name by any chance Hackney, Daughter of Tower-Hamlets?'

Jack tried to swallow, but his throat was dry. 'Yes' he squeaked. 'Mummy's name is Hackney. She's gone to Ibeefa for a holiday.'

The giant regarded Jack with inquisitive eyes – eyes that grew increasingly rheumy as the moment wore on. The pub dogs both put down their sewing, the better to watch the drama unfolding. The short-sighted one popped his specs on his nose. The pub's cat, as fat as a pot-bellied pig fed on a small saucer called 'Demand', took a box of tissues from behind the bar and went over to sit between the dogs, tugging out a tissue for each of them and one for himself.

'I didn't go away, son – your mother wanted a divorce and the Family Court wouldn't let me have any visitation rights. Put a restraining order in place so that I couldn't even come within *seeing you* distance. I've been paying child support these past twenty-five years.'

'Daddy? Are *you* my Daddy?'

Both pub dogs, in their baskets near the fireplace, dabbed tears of emotion from their eyes. They were big softies at heart. The pub cat wasn't quite at the point of crying yet and so stuck one back leg in the air and licked his anus.

'Yes, son' confirmed Dagenham, wondering how a hug might be achieved but concluding sadly that under the circumstances of the disparity in physical development then presiding such a manoeuvre as a father-son hug was too dangerous to attempt. Dagenham, after a long, long short while, addressed the landlord. 'A pint for my son, if you please, landlord, and whatever you're having. In fact – a round of drinks on me. Pints for everyone!'

A great roar went up and a great many vast tankards were swiftly emptied. The commotion at the bar allowed the reunion to take place in a more human, less public, sub-setting. 'Phew, thank the Greek & Roman gods for that' said the author.

The landlord lent Dagenham his jeweller's loupe so that he could see the little passport-sized photograph of his mother that Jack produced. 'Yep, that's her alright.'

Jack feared that his loyalties, tatters such as they were, would be tested by a tirade of marital criticism, but Dagenham had learnt a thing or two in his wilderness years, and he remained circumspect on the matter. It would take not some little time for Jack and his father to acquaint themselves.

'Beautiful as the day I took her up the bus shelter. Face an angelic cross between Princess Anne and Les Dawson, body like the love-child of Hattie Jacques and a JCB. It was like shagging a cart-horse over an electric fence. Best one minute and fifteen seconds of my entire sex life' said Dagenham, lost in his memories, lost in space, and time – and meaning.

A kind of hush settled, not all over the world, but just around their little group, and all that could be heard was the pub dogs and cat blubbing. It eventually became a tad awkward.

'Game o'darts?' suggested Bert, thinking correctly that a distraction was exactly what was needed, paradoxically, to allow the two to focus on the matter in hand.

Jack though was not much larger than the darts, half the weight of a dart, and the board, for him, was a good five minutes' walk away from the line and sixty foot up a wall.

'Hmm. You've got a point there, if you'll pardon the pun. Let me think now. Aha! Football. That's the thing' said Sidney. 'Game of football with the lads.'

Jack began to protest about being smaller than the ball and hinting at worries that an ill-judged kick might be squishy-fatal. Perhaps, he suggested, he could just be a goalpost or one of those chaps who runs up and down with a flag on the sidelines or something? If they could find him a little broom he could do that frantic brush-brush thing in front of the ball to make sure that the ice was clean.

The sight of the giant-sized Subbuteo table allayed most, if not all, of Jack's fears. At least he could move up and down the table whereas the other players could only move from side to side. Jack quite forgot himself, hung his new jacket up on one of the goal-posts, and had some pure and unadulterated, guilt-free fun. The best kick-about – the *only* kick-about – of his life to date. Who won the match? Nobody knew, nobody cared, for that was never the point. At the end of the match they'd all bonded more securely than a hunting party of meerkats given a bag of zip-ties to play with and then sprayed with Super-Glue.

This being a special occasion of course, the pub had a lock-in and it was beyond three of the morning when Jack fell asleep on the bar under a Guinness towel, his head on a packet of salted peanuts. When Jack woke he was surrounded by giants among men, sleeping off the effects of seven or eight gallons of beer each, and only the pub dogs noticed that he was awake, acknowledging him with a desultory wag of the tail. He scanned the crowd.

They were all so ...solid. Jack had always avoided draughts in case they blew him over, but this lot looked as though they could wrestle a tornado and then strangle the cloud it rode into town on. They'd all spoken to him during the evening – spoken to him nicely, not reading out the list of charges or giving him a lecture on how he could never, never, never really atone for his privilege as a pale, stale, male man man-cub. Every one of them had some sort of profession or business. None of that *Tinker Tailor Soldier Sailor Rich-man Poor-man Beggar-man Thief* rubbish either. This lot were blacksmiths, lumberjacks, train-drivers, miners, farmers with real farms (not just one sad old cow), firemen, policemen, giant wandering poets, bus drivers, brick-layers, road sweepers, steel-workers and all manner of other fancy professions such as giant doctors and giant dentists and veterinarians looking after what must be some amazingly large animals such as three-foot high hedgehogs and stuff. Even the ones who were 'tween jobs were still part of the gang and nobody took the piss out of them for having to sign on at the Giant Labour Exchange.

Jack lay warm, if slightly beer-damp and peanut-salty, on the bar and reflected on his own life. What, he wondered, could he turn his own hand to, with his excellent Bachelorette's Degree Diploma Participation Certificate from the *No Failures Here Everyone's a Winner University of Scunthorpe* in "Gender Studies and Feminism and Victimhood Observed Necessarily Remotely by the Bastard Guilty Modern Male in a Post-Empire Self-Identified Omni-Fluidity; Feelz Trump Facts Every Time."

Think and think and think though he thought, "sod all" was the answer he came to. As Bert had commented sometime during the evening; might as well wipe your arse on that certificate, my lad.

Talking of which, the time had come the walrus said. Not even contemplating tackling the immense porcelain fitments in the Gents – he'd seen and been terrified by the gutter for the communal urinal - Jack made good use of an ashtray and then made as-suggested use of his degree certificate. The little bit of blue ribbon and the embossed gold snowflake proved to be a bit scratchy, but he was beginning to toughen up in spite of himself. He washed his hands under a soda-siphon, the unexpectedly strong flow nearly landing him in the drip tray under the SodBucket's Old Peculiar, Bishop's Todger and Arkwright's Badger's Nutsack pumps.

Jack's eyes fell on his father, snoring loudly into the coal scuttle. Jack's father had told him that he was a lumberjack. Now that would be a great career but could he cut it? No pun in ten did. Jack looked at his own arms – it was true, the long climb up the soy-beanstalk had begun to produce a few very satisfying bulges where some work-a-day muscles ought to be. The food in giant-land *was* filling him out so that he no longer looked like a joke xylophone propped up on two sticks. Jack turned over to lie on his side, his head propped up on his hand. It would be a bit of a cliché though, following in your father's footsteps (even if it currently took ten steps for Jack to cross one of his father's). Perhaps ...a tree surgeon? The same, but different, sort of building on what his Dad did. Then he could say things like 'My Dad taught me everything I knowed, and I founded out all of the rest for myself.'

Hmm.

First things first though. If he was going to do this his own way, by himself, then he had to get back down that ruddy beanstalk and get himself into Tree Surgeon College. Were there such places? Dad would know.

Now *there* was a phrase that warmed Jack's cockles. *Dad would know.* Settling back down under the bar-towel for a bit of a lie-in, Jack decided that he'd ask his Dad for some advice when he woke up.

Victoria Frankenstein's Positively Adorable Monster

The Almighty moves in mysterious ways His wonders to perform.

My ways *My* wonders to perform I have documented and detailed for any and all to follow and repeat, as a competent scientist records her successes.

Once upon a time the Almighty was wholly unique in reserving unto Himself the gift of Life. I have, by painstaking study and logical, scientific feelz and feminine intuition, given unto myself that trifling power, and I am now standing shoulder to shoulder with God. Slightly taller, if anything, because I am in heels. Anything God can do *I* can do in heels.

I could walk out onto any battlefield among the smoke and the blood and the ruins and cause a fallen army of men to rise up to fight again on my behalf and to do a proper job with their second chance. Perhaps one day I will do so, and then we shall what the Almighty, faded and reduced by the passage of time, has in *His* box of paltry replies. What a glorious battle that would be!

By alchemy and by chemistry and by the precise application of controlled deep emotion I can cause life where before lay only life's absence.

Some say that God is dead, killed by Progress. *I* say that *if* God *is* dead then it is of no cause for alarm. Bring His body to me in my laboratory, and I will set the matter right!

No, I say that God lives yet. He watched me at my work. The Almighty will doubtless consider me a comfort, knowing now that we have but to remain on good terms for Him to never fear death again!

God began his work humbly with light and with clay - I too began my elevation on the most humble of terms, working night and – no, actually just night, never day – with the earthworms and with the creeping, crawling things (unwanted small children; scullery maids; suffragettes of the *lower* classes with neither friend not relative to report them missing).

God, lacking ambition, began His career with the creation of a mere Man – I begin mine with the creation of the ultimate - a *Woman*! I cannot abide nor will *I* tolerate half measures.

The future is *Female*!

The future is *Me*male!

The name of Victoria Frankenstein shall light the firmament for all of eternity! Ah ha ha ha.

Unless I decide to revert to my own "maiden" name, in which case the name of Victoria *Sponge* shall light the firmament for all of eternity! Ah ha ha ha.

Daddy was a Master Baker, according to Mummy.

Anyway, what*ever*.

I have become my own star, looking down upon all things, understanding all things, imbued with the ultimate knowledge. I may say in all modesty; Look upon *my* works, ye mighty, and despair.

My own dear family looked first upon my works and, frankly, they seemed to be none too chuffed with them.

Some several weeks past our dear family pussy-cat, The Lady Belladonna, as she slept peacefully in the roadway, was deliberately and brutally murdered by a *man* driving a brewer's dray. Men are *all* cat-haters, aren't they? Four Shire horses, four iron-rimmed wooden wheels and twenty-four barrels of dark ale defeated our beloved companion animal and left her dead, in the gutter. Also stuck on the rims of two of the wheels, and with some of her vitals hanging on the wrought iron gate of the house opposite. These organs probably squirted out when she was squashed.

I had the man flogged in the street of course by some other men, and to within an inch of his life, but this did nothing to console poor Abstemia and Disapprobation, my dear darling daughters. A plan formed then in my mind much as a town fog swirls and forms spirit shapes that chase us from late carriage to doorway lantern. The Way Ahead became clear to me. I resolved, as a Woman, to embark upon a Plan of Action – to bring my Science into the world! To add to the light of Creation! Where Mother Nature's healing processes were overwhelmed a little, my *science* would win *Me* the day!

Quietly, and without fuss, I called upon the services of my couturier, my coiffurist, my Feng Shui advisor, my Tarot reader, my shoe-maker, my lace-maker, my dressmaker, my milliner *modiste*, and my lady's maids. I slipped on my laboratory gloves. Well, I held my hands out, and my India-rubber gloves were slipped on me. Same thing, really. God, how I *love* the aroma of warm rubber!

The promise of a ha'penny a piece was quietly issued to the local street-urchin boys, and thus I was gathered the mortal remains of The Lady Belladonna in secret unto my laboratory in the second-best potting shed (the attic is already in use on some silly and frivolous project of my husband's doing, and the cardoon seedlings are doing quite well in the *best* potting shed and so must not be moved).

Each night for two weeks I slaved beyond ordinary human endurance, between the hours of nine-thirty pm and ten-thirty pm, with only the shortest of breaks and with bailing twine and metal clips and scullery clothes-pegs and - most of all - with my Scientific Feelings.

On the fourteenth inst I was encouraged in my endeavours by the ever-curious Almighty with a thunderstorm of quite the sweetest duration and intensity. *He* obviously approved of my work! Terrified, ignorant, and smouldering slightly from the effects of a residual voltage in the capacitor bank, my laboratory assistant, Igorina, raised the electrical mast high, high into the clouds, almost as high as the shuttered windows on the first floor of our town-house (she was standing on two large books piled high on a chair).

I remember her ridiculous protestations quite clearly.

'It's pronounced "*Eeeegoreeena*" actually ma'am.'

I gave her my very best "and I would care for why?" look. Mere functionaries do get so beyond themselves these days. This one was electrically-damaged and it was still giving lip!

My eyes intent upon my work, I raised my rubber-handled iron probes over Belladonna on the slab and I waited for the sky to give me the required fifty-thousand amp-volty-wattings of sparky-sparky lightning-juice, and at the proper moment I achieved insertion! One probe in the cat's mouth, the other where the sun was often eclipsed by dust raised in her litter tray.

Lady Belladonna fizzed and buzzed and crackled and twitched, and one or two of her sutures popped, the gas lights in the houses up and down the avenue dimmed and guttered as the gas voltage dropped briefly, Igorina screamed and my cat lived again, and lived with a vitality hitherto unseen in a big, fat, salmon-and-cream-fed Persian long-hair whose idea of exercise was to stand up to shit.

Oh, how pleased the girls would be with me!

I determined to re-introduce The Lady Belladonna at breakfast the next day, after she had enjoyed a good night's sleep in a soothing vat of warm embalming fluid enriched by Bubbles of the Common Breathing-Gases (I borrowed that pumpy-pumpy bubble thing from Victor's silly rare tropical fish tank).

Well, in spite of breakfast being the most important meal of the day, Victor came out with most profane language, right over the kedgeree and the devilled kidneys. He barked about some of his precious fish floating on the surface. I replied that it was nice that they were learning new tricks and asked what it was that he was teaching the other fish, swimming through hoops or swimming in circles perhaps?

Had he but previously shown the slightest interest in my work he would have known that the anatomically unlikely solo scenario that he positively *shouted* out loud was not then totally *without* my grasp. I was glad that at least the servants would not understand his *Greek* expostulations to: 'bugger me sideways with a badger' and 'what the hell have you done now, you silly, silly, cow?'

The girls, Abstemia and Disapprobation, busy tearing into their soft-boiled breakfast larks, did not at first notice my triumph, being seated with their backs towards me. I set The Lady Belladonna upon the table between them, quite near to the quince marmalade.

'Look, darlings! Mummy's brought kitty-witty back to life!'

The Lady Belladonna's remaining eye chose that unfortunate moment to unseat itself and dangle on the optic nerve, and the cat was not yet in full possession of her meow, issuing instead a sort of low, watery gargle-growl that sounded for all the world as though she was speaking!

K-k-k-illl me. K-k-k-ill me now, f-f-f-for the love of God... kkkjjqqelssrrggghhmeh, or some such figment. Then she coughed something up. I think it may have been part of her spinal column. Cats are *so* funny!

I propped her jauntily against the toast rack and smoothed down her fur, which was still on the wild side of "upright" after her electro-chemical adventures. Lead-acid batteries and domestic cats ought never to be mixed unless, like me, you're an expert with both, and know exactly what you're doing. It was only then that I noticed that I had amusingly confused a front and rear leg during the re-attaching process, and The Lady Belladonna wouldn't be her usual elegant self again until I'd made some very minor further repairs. Still, she *could* then turn on the proverbial sixpence. Every liver has a silver lining, as we bio-scientists say!

Abstemia and Disapprobation left the breakfast room via the French windows. It is fortunate in a way that due to my husband's manifold financial inadequacies we are not yet double-glazed, or else the girls might have suffered concussion and a cranial confounding rather than – I assume – just minor cuts. The aspidistra by the small piano wobbled a little in its pot and then fell over. Really, the *drama* was quite ridiculous.

My precious baby girls (Abstemia just sixteen, Disapprobation just seventeen) were brought back to me by the authorities after a day or so, although as with The Lady Belladonna, neither of them has yet spoken a coherent word. Apparently they were found under the altar of the local church, subsisting on sacramental wine and wafers and chain-smoking their way through the stolen cigarettes hidden under there. It was the smoke during a service that led to their discovery, and to the charging of the Priest for receiving and handling.

Upon return the dear things stood in the hallway, staring into every corner with wide eyes, and they trembled when I hugged them and ordered them immediately to bed with a glass of warm buttermilk and a dish of cold sardines each. There's little better for raising the spirits.

Children just never appreciate the wonders of Science until much later in life, do they?

I learned later that the girls had asked their father, Victor, to put the cat out of their misery. Victor clubbed The Lady Belladonna to pieces, and those he buried in a mirror-finished steel-lined box in consecrated ground. He did not tell the girls that he had been unable to actually (re-)kill the cat; the pieces lived on whatever he did to them. Fire would have brought an end to the matter, but he couldn't bring himself to that. Men are such cowards, aren't they? Stupid, too.

When the fuss had subsided I ordered Igorina to dig up Belladonna's remains, and to burn them in the house's centralised heating boiler's fire. Oh how we laughed – a good cat just can't help but make a home seem warmer, one way or another, can it?

Society would have expected the reaction of my family to bring about an end to my work, and for me to return to being the demure little housewife and mother who held wonderful tea parties and performed exhaustingly good works for half a day twice monthly during the summer season. It did not. Their unthinking, unreasoned, brutish and ignorant responses spurred me on to ever-greater efforts, although they did bring about a severe chill in our family relations.

Chilling them was important, because for my greatest project, for my opus magnum, for a creation the size and complexity and sophistication of *Woman*, I would need time, and the flesh does suffer putrefaction so very, very swiftly if certain measures are not taken in the period *after* donation but *before* re-animation.

They had ridiculed and belittled my work. Well, they were all but Abstemia laughing on the other side of their faces when I'd finished clubbing them to death as they slept. I preserved Abstemia's little face from damage most carefully, it being quite the sweetest of the family, and the face that my creation would wear when presented to the world. Mother, of course, never really sleeps, but her confinement to a wheelchair made her dispatch a mere matter of chasing around the best withdrawing room for five minutes until I managed to get her cornered near the larger piano forte. May the Greek and Roman gods bless her, it took six or seven good swipes with my hammer before she finally stopped playing 'Abide with me'.

You see, I wanted my creation to have the very best possible start in life.

Note to self: remember to have the wheelchair disentangled from the piano and to have the instrument professionally re-tuned.

Where was I? Oh yes – the very best start in life.

I selected the torso, the arms and legs and right hand of Victor, my husband, for strength. The face, the dear, sweet, innocent face of Abstemia, the face that could be denied nothing by any man, for beauty. The delicate feet and the left hand of Disapprobation, for her nimble step, and for delicate work. The auburn hair of my mother, for temperament, and her brain, for the feminine traits. Mother was the very embodiment of gentleness, unconditional love, empathy, and even-temperament – it is from her that I myself inherited those qualities. Oh – and the breasts of Harcourt, my personal lady's maid, whose voluptuous and pendulous glands I had admired for many, many years (nipples like cathedral door-knobs). Sadly Harcourt came upon me during the early stages of my work – the stages involving the various saws, and the hammer and chisels – and she could not stop screaming. At least I didn't need her head.

My creation would have the best of everything, and with me as teacher, the best possible chance in life too. As well as the finest body that may be devised she will have in addition my personal philosophy of life, such as it is.

Never forget, never forgive, take what you want, when you want it, leave someone else to pay the bill. Never look back, never regret, never doubt that you're worth it. If Judgement ever catches you up, turn on the tears, come up with any old bullshit for an excuse, and they'll let you off with a hug and twenty-five guineas from public funds to ease your obvious trauma. The world is run by men, and men are thick and easily manipulated. You go girl!

Igorina and I – with me in a purely supervisory role, natch – dressed my creation in the finest couture available. An XXXXL 'This is what a feminist looks like' t-shirt by

Ye Olde Sweat Shoppe of Delhi, denim dungarees by B&Q, worn with one buckle unfastened. Igorina, blessed love that she is, quickly crocheted a hat in pink wool, from a design pattern that made both of us blush. Oh, we played with it certainly – *neep neep!* – but it made us blush.

The temperature in the laboratory ice-room must have been a little higher than might have been desirable, for Abstemia's lips, however we stitched and riveted them, developed and maintained a constant sneer. Her large, round, thick-rimmed spectacles still fitted though, even over dear Mother's elephantine ears. There was a little too much of the "teenage Swedish whining eco-misery brat" about the whole facial ensemble really, but one works with what one has. Let's face it (pun intended), at eight foot tall and half that wide no-one is going to tell *my* creation to "shut up, annoying little girl, and get back to school", are they?

Self-Satisfied Smug-Smiley emoticons r us.

I did so hope that my creation would be able to self-satisfy too. It would be the Devil's own problem coming up with an appropriately sized dildo-on-legs (man), if not. Who in their right mind would want to spend time stitching a *man* together! Ugh! Slugs and snails and puppy-dog's tails, and other squelchy items, that's what men are made of.

Skin is difficult to work with even in the best of circumstances, and under the gas lights appeared to have become translucent, and to have developed an almost nicotine-yellow hue. Dear Victor's musculature, veins and arteries showed through like a map of the new and *genuinely* insane "Underground Railway" network. On a positive note, at least this made it easy to check that the blood was flowing properly. Ba-dum; squish, ba-dum; squish. One didn't so much *take* the pulse rate as one followed it up and down the arm.

These minor flaws though are hardly the point. Mother's brain, once re-animated, functioned beautifully, and her first action was to test her own motor co-ordination and strength. She reached up from the table and throttled Igorina. How clever of my creation to awake in her new situation and to immediately enter self-test mode AND to address the problem of spare parts supply.

Between us we woman-handled Igorina into the ice-room.

Chuckles did most of the work.

Chuckles is what I named my creation.

There remained one difficult problem for me to solve. Where ought one best to unveil the result of such a magnificent scientific breakthrough? What sober scientific institution would be best? In what forum might the highest number of my inferiors best be able to gain access to my data? Now does one introduce completely new life to the everyday, commonplace, real world?

I decided upon Oxbridge.

The little village of Oxbridge has a duck pond, a public house and a highly respected polytechnic specialising in *Naturist Feminism and Practical Hands-On Gender Studies*.

Chuckles would make her debut appearance during the "no platform" demonstrations related to a planned talk about some supposed "empathy gap" delivered by some old academic fossil, who would doubtless be male, pale and stale and ought thus to have been done away with years ago. We would blend in with the crowd, engage in some light bonding and then I would requisition a microphone and reveal to the whole world how special Chuckles really was! How delighted and surprised they would be!

With her stunning physical presence and her quicksilver mind (at room temperature and above) Chuckles had so much more to bring to the show than merely a musty, cadaverous odour and a tendency to leak amber and green-coloured fluids from the most surprising of places. I was certain that everyone would be kind and understanding in these matters, as am I, always, whatever someone else's foibles.

One ought never to stoop to the ad hominem and in especially so in the matter of immutable characteristics. Academics grow to be male, pale and stale by choice (they always have the better option of crawling away into some dark corner and remaining out of the public eye), but my creature was pale and a little stale because of *Science*, not because of *Patriarchal Privilege*.

My faith was rewarded.

Armed with two large pots of low-fat soya pro-biotic yoghurt, one raspberry flavour, one cherry nut cola flavour, with which to present our reasoned arguments at the demonstration, Chuckles and I hove up to the crowd. Silence fell, one might have heard a hairpin drop, had any of the ladies there present been familiar with such an instrument of oppression. The last of the window glass tinkled to the ground and an awed hush descended.

Chuckles was *out in the world*!

How proud I was. I could not have been any more prouderer. It was not quite the gentle blending in that I had hoped for, but even at a no-platform demo there was butch - and then there was Chuckles.

Chuckles tugged aside her dungarees top to show her "This is what a feminist looks like" sweatshop tee and the crowd rushed forward as one, pick-axe handles held high, un-leaded low-emission re-usable flaming brands held aloft. The crowd screamed, oh how they screamed!

Chuckles had never been hugged before, and certainly not hugged so enthusiastically, and by a crowd comprised of one hundred percent Feminist, seventy-eight percent Lesbian or Bi-Curious, thirty-nine percent BAME, twelve percent Alternatively Enabled (Wheelchair, Crutch and/or Assistance Animal users), twenty-two and one half percent

Religion of Peace, eleven percent left-handed, eighty-one percent BMI Outliers and ninety-three percent domestic and/or general abuse survivors, ninety-seven percent of whom were Women and three percent were Guest Feminists-With-(Small, Relatively-Inoffensive, Unused)-Penises and/or Supporters Of The Glorious Cause take a breath, breathe, phuphox ache, your brain is going to implode yeah?

Unable to contain myself I jizz-handed with glee!

Damn those patriarchal predictive text autocorrects, just damn them all to Hell!

I, of course, *jazz* handed with glee. Trust *something* male to spoil the moment.

Such a magical, heart-warming moment (re-animated heart tissue does need to be kept slightly warmer than might be usual, feminist group hugging being quite the best way of achieving this).

One of Mother's ears dropped off, putting Chuckles' spectacles at an unfortunate angle. It mattered not.

The male security staff of the polytechnic were not equipped to deal with such an harmonious outpouring of unconditional feminine achievement and love and togetherness and love and success and happiness and love and reason and logic and philosophical laissez-fair happy-go-lucky inclusivity.

'AAARRGGHH! IT'S A MONSTER!' shouted one of them as he backed away.

Men, threatened by *any* gathering of Strong Women, have always dismissed *all* such Women as "monsters" of society. Why *do* men always feel the need to reduce strong and independent women to floods of tears by calling them horrid names?

The Police were called of course by campus security, and the security man who had shouted the nasty Hate Speech was arrested and put in hand-cuffs and thrown into the Police Paddy Wagon... um, the Police Black Maria...

um, the Police *Carriage*. The Police Person Officer Person assured the traumatised demonstrators that the horrible man would be put away for a very long time where he couldn't hurt anybody else.

'Where's that then, Parliament?' asked one wag of indeterminate gender from the shadows.

'No, gaol' came the immediate and simply hilarious, humour-filled reply from the CPS Field Representative for Immediate Feminist Justice for Women Hurt by Men. 'Parliament is the seat of such government as we currently have in England. It is not a recognised penal institution and were he to be sent there we would only have to remove him to a nearby gaol. To move the miscreant twice would not be logical.'

A roar of visceral approval went up from the protestors.

Chuckles had strangled someone.

It was the man who had called her a monster.

Chuckles had torn the roof off the police carriage, lifted the man out, chains and all, and pulled him limb from limb until she felt better about herself.

An ambulance was called, and it clattered up over the cobbles behind six high-speed horses, the blue-glass oil-lamps being rotated by small boys strapped to the roof for that purpose.

Chuckles was gently seated in the ambulance, everyone respecting her emergency emotional disarray.

Chuckles was offered a delicious, calming cocktail of Diazepam, Lorazepam, Mogadon and Smirnoff BAME, shaken over ice and served stirred with a bar of pink chocolate shaped like a clitoris.

'The bastard! You were provoked beyond human endurance!' said the Police Person Officer Person making up Chuckles' statement on her behalf, not wanting to add to her stress and upset by forcing her to speak for herself. 'You felt physically threatened and you only walked over to the Police carriage, tore off the roof, pulled the man out, chains and all, from between his guards and killed him because that was the only way you could defend yourself' the Police Person continued, adding a few stars and a little love-heart with an arrow through it in the margin, to lighten things. 'You have a sweet and gentle nature, even though you come from a broken family.'

'Don't you mean "a broken home"?' asked the Sergeantess, reading over the Police Constabull's shoulder, not realising that the Police Constabull had already talked to Victoria who had explained a few bits and pieces. Mostly Victor's bits, Abstemia and Disapprobation's pieces, Victoria's mother's odds and sods and, of course, the screaming lady's maid's magnificent tits with the nipples like cathedral door-knobs.

The Police Person Officeress Constabull thought a little, licked her pencil (a horrid, phallic, habit indicating past intellectual and emotional damage due to forced fellatio, no doubt) and added 'When you defended yourself against the man by unavoidably accidentally unintentionally understandably killing him to a totally natural death by good causes you were not *entirely* yourself.'

This much was indeed true.

There had to be a show-trial of course, the public would accept no less.

The nasty, obviously guilty man's remains were stacked up in plastic bags in the dock for the duration. The prosecution read out the man's history to the court and to the press gallery – he had a long history of being a man – and this, although ruled inadmissible by the Judge (after it had been read) may have influenced the jury, who found him guilty on some twelve of the ten charges against him. Convicted of being male, pale, binary, insufficiently ethnic, rude, horrid, misogynistic, colonialist, homophobic, homophonic, guilty of receiving higher pay than a woman – and also really quite ugly, he was sentenced in sentient absentia to life imprisonment on each charge, the sentences

142

to run consecutively or one after the other, whichever would be longest.

Chuckles was awarded fifty hundred guineas from the Public Purse as a gesture to help her recover from the experience.

There was some silly talk in the gutter tabloids about Victoria pursuing her creation into the Arctic Circle, away from huwomanity, so that no further killy-killings would take place, but this was just press misogyny piled upon press misogyny.

Victoria and Chuckles instead embarked upon a lecture tour of the New World, appearances including speaking to the League of Nations and on the White House Lawn where Chuckles chided the President of The Colony for terming it the *White* House, and not something more inclusive, such as the *Black* House – for we are all of us black, at heart.

For Victoria the highlight of the tour – aside from the many large bags of folding moolah coming their way – was meeting a little girl called "Greta", who often explained to everyone all about climate and *she* felt that it had all been stolen and ruined and destroyed and broken a lot by icky old people who would all be dead from old age soon anyway and who just wanted to steal the future from Children because children were young, yeah?

With Chuckles and Greta standing side by side, pouting and frowning, everyone was put in mind of their being two "Russian Dolls", just with twenty or thirty of the intervening set missing. Oh how everyone laughed (except for Greta, who was not laughing-enabled).

Guffaw guffaw guffaw.

Victoria and Chuckles were aboard ship and bound for Scandinavia by the time the First Lady's body was found, and there was no evidence at all other than purely circumstantial finger-prints and a little bit of DNA and fifteen eye-witnesses to link Chuckles to the tragedy. Some suggested that only Chuckles would have been capable of strangling the First Lady at the waist instead of the more usual strangulation-of-the-neck, but this was a horrid thing to say because only men were violent and Chuckles was a *girl*.

So it was that the pair ended up in Stockholm, which is *almost* the Arctic Circle, and had been able to give little Greta a carboniferous-neutral lift home, in their crow's nest or fo'c's'le or bilges or something. Anyway, her Mummy and Daddy were very worried about her being out in a changeable climate without her ABBA dolls and fresh bobbles for her hair plaits, and they whisked her away for a restorative all-naked Jacuzzi thing with everyone else from her home town including the mayor and a man called Lars who self-identified as a reindeer and chanted traditional Sámi folk songs rather than speaking in the more usual manner.

The Swede-like Port Authorities, being *men* and being obsessed with silly details, wanted to know all about why the ship had sailed from New York with fifty members of crew and arrived in Stockholm with only thirty. Chuckles, who by then had learned a thing or two, smoothed down her dress, crossed (Victor's, hairy-) legs to show a touch of thigh and wept into a handkerchief, explaining that it had been a rough voyage and she'd really like to get to her hotel as soon as possible please before she was overcome with... *WOMEN'S PROBLEMS*. Go Chuckles! Put those men off their guard! Flash that Get Out Of Gaol Free card!

The Stockholmish were very nice people, really, and even a bit like the Amish, although the Stockholmishers' name was much longer and they all drove Volvo 144 estates or Saab 99 saloons, both of course with winter tyres and driveway driver-preheat.

In Stockholm, in a glittering ceremony (with glitter fountains and lots of ceremony), Victoria was awarded the Nobel Prize for Alchemy. Also for Needlework, and for Not Only Surviving The Trauma of Losing Her Husband

And Daughters To Tragedy, But Positively Thriving After Losing Her Husband And Daughters To Tragedy.

That last one took quite a bit of cunning engraving to fit onto the little Silver Cup.

Chuckles was awarded a Nobel Prize for *Everything Else*, and was then named as Ambassador to The League of Nations for Women's Equality, Gendered Violence & Toxic Masculinity.

Chuckles, upon hearing of the award, threw her hands up in the air in delight, but these were later stitched back on by the First Aid Nurse at the venue. The First Aid Nurse was later found concealed behind the First Aid caravan. Also behind the venue's wheelie bins, and under some parked Volvo 144 estates and Saab 99 saloons in the venue car park. She/Shey must have been tragically murdered by man or men unknown soon after treating Chuckles' injuries. *'Bastards! How many more women must be murdered to death by men before we can kill all men to stop them murdering women?'* said the Chief of Police, Gotha Killemalle.

Victoria's speech re-iterated her self-nominated position as a new goddess, equal in all ways to the Almighty – better, in fact, in having the natural empathy and intuition and sensitivity and self-control and modesty of a Modern Feminist Woman.

Pope Gerald, on behalf of the Catholic Church, expressed mild misgivings from the front row of the audience about Victoria's self-elevation, and was promptly told to shut up because, as a man, he had no say in the matter, and anyway, did he really want to face capital charges of "Belittling the achievements of a Woman in Science, contrary to the Public Interest"?

Pope Gerald said that he'd rather not face such charges, if it was all the same, and he apologised on behalf of God, and retracted his statement.

A small-circulation English comic labouring under the title of "Private Eye" hinted at being in possession of laboratory notebooks proving that Victoria had in fact just been following her husband Victor's laboratory notes when she had created the creature, that it had in fact been *he* who had first re-animated matter and that Victor had, in fact, already created a man-monster from human scraps and off-cuts before Victoria had even set up her laboratory in the second-best potting shed. Their offices were sadly burned to the ground, but not before the entire staff apparently went insane and dismembered one another. Nobody could come up with a plausible theory as to how the last man alive might have pulled his own limbs and head off, but there you go, male violence knows no bounds does it?

Victoria patented the process for the Creation of Life, was awarded unlimited Legal Aid, and is currently suing God for infringement of her patent and for punitive damages relating to commercial gains accruing from the creation of eleventy-twelve million souls.

Chuckles lives a quiet life in a small house in the Whitechapel district of London, and enjoys needlework, her cat, and stitching her cat back together after periods when her medication balance had been less than optimum and/or she'd forgotten her own strength.

Victoria and Chuckles remain, to this day, classic examples of an oppressed minority.

They all lived happily ever after, although TBH, anyone who criticises them *does not*.

The End.

About The Author

Born during tiffin in the sea-side town of Cleethorpes, England, in nineteen-sixty. Whole family immediately moved to Hong Kong where Father worked for the Ministry of Defence, spying on Cold-War Red China by listening in to their radio transmissions. Hutson Minor spoke only Cantonese and some pidgin English and was a complete brat.

At the end of the sixties was to be found on the Isle of Lewis in the Outer Hebrides of Scotland. Still a brat. There finally learned to read and write under the strict disciplinarian regime of the Nicolson Institute and one Miss Crichton. Then spent a year living in Banham Zoo in Norfolk, swapping childhood imaginary friends for howler monkeys, penguins.

Followed, for want of something better to do and for want of a brain, in Daddy's footsteps and found himself working for the British Civil Service in areas much too foul to be named. Was eventually asked to leave by the Home Secretary. A few years of corporate life earned some more kind invitations to leave. Ran a few businesses, several limited companies, then went down the plug-hole with the global economy and found himself in court, bankrupt with home, car and valuables auctioned off by H.M. Official Receivers. Lived for a long time by candlelight in a hedgerow in rural Lincolnshire as a peacenik vegan hippie drop-out, darning old socks and living on fresh air and a sense of the ridiculous. Moved thence to living on a narrowboat on England's canal network, still living on fresh air and an increased sense of the ridiculous.

Dog person not a cat person. Favourite colours include faded tangerine and cobalt blue. Fatally allergic to

Penicillin and very nearly so to Jerusalem Artichokes. Loves coffee and loves curry. Has tried his hardest all of his life to ride bicycles but simply looks like a deranged, overweight orang-utan on wheels. Favourite film Blade Runner (original only). Uses the word "splendid" far too much. Splendid.

Other books by this author

Cheerio, and thanks for the apocalypse

The Cat Wore Electric Goggles (not about cats)

The Dog With The Bakelite Nose (not about dogs)

Narrowboat Winter 2020 Three Named Storms and a Pandemic

Printed in Poland
by Amazon Fulfillment
Poland Sp. z o.o., Wrocław

57616585R00089